ARMY BOYS ON GERMAN SOIL

Our Doughboys Quelling the Mobs

HOMER RANDALL

1st WORLD
LIBRARY
Literary Society

Army Boys on German Soil

Homer Randall

© 1st World Library, 2008
PO Box 2211
Fairfield, IA 52556
www.1stworldlibrary.com
First Edition

LCCN: 2007935390

Softcover ISBN: 978-1-4218-9339-6
Hardcover ISBN: 978-1-4218-9439-3
eBook ISBN: 978-1-4218-9239-9

Purchase *"Army Boys on German Soil"*
as a traditional bound book at:
www.1stWorldLibrary.com/purchase.asp?ISBN=978-1-4218-9339-6

1st World Library is a literary, educational organization
dedicated to:

- Creating a free internet library of downloadable ebooks

- Hosting writing competitions and offering book publishing
scholarships.

Interested in more 1st World Library books? contact:
literacy@1stworldlibrary.com
Check us out at: www.1stworldlibrary.com

1ˢᵗ World Library Literary Society

Giving Back to the World

"If you want to work on the core problem, it's early school literacy."

- James Barksdale, former CEO of Netscape

"No skill is more crucial to the future of a child, or to a democratic and prosperous society, than literacy."

- Los Angeles Times

"Literacy... means far more than learning how to read and write... The aim is to transmit... knowledge and promote social participation."

- UNESCO

"Literacy is not a luxury, it is a right and a responsibility. If our world is to meet the challenges of the twenty-first century we must harness the energy and creativity of all our citizens."

- President Bill Clinton

"Parents should be encouraged to read to their children, and teachers should be equipped with all available techniques for teaching literacy, so the varying needs and capacities of individual kids can be taken into account."

- Hugh Mackay

CONTENTS

CHAPTER I

THE FLASH FROM THE GUNS

"I tell you, Bart, I don't like the looks of things," remarked Frank Sheldon to his chum, Bart Raymond, as the two stood on a corner in the German city of Coblenz on the Rhine.

"What's on your mind?" inquired Bart, as he drew the collar of his raincoat more snugly around his neck and turned his back to the sleet-laden wind that was fairly blowing a gale. "I don't see anything to get stirred up about except this abominable weather. It's all I can do to keep my feet."

"It is a pretty tough night to be out on patrol duty," agreed Frank. "But it wasn't that I was thinking about. It's the way these Huns have been acting lately."

"Are you thinking of that sergeant of ours that was found stabbed to death the other night?" asked Bart, with quickened interest.

"Not so much that," replied Frank, "although that's one of the things that shows the way the wind is blowing. But it's the surly way the whole population is acting. Haven't you noticed it?"

"There certainly is a difference," admitted Bart. "Everything was peaches and cream when we first came. The people fairly fell over themselves in trying to tell us how glad they were to have the Americans here instead of the French and English. Now they're getting chesty again. A couple of fellows passed me a little while ago who looked at me as if they'd like to slip a knife into me if they dared."

"They hate us all right," declared Frank. "It makes them sore as the mischief to have Americans keeping the watch on the Rhine. They're mad enough to bite nails every time they're reminded of it."

"And that's pretty often," laughed Bart, "for they can't go out into the street without seeing an American uniform some-where. We've got this old town pretty well policed, and if any trouble starts we'll put it down in a jiffy."

"Well, trouble's coming all right," prophesied Frank. "There are lots of new faces in the city, fellows who seem to have come from the outside. You know Germany's being ripped up the back everywhere by mobs, and the red flag is flying in Berlin. I have a hunch that these outsiders have come to start the same thing here."

"If they do they'll get more than they bargained for," said Bart grimly. "They'll find they're monkeying with a buzz saw. What our fellows would do to them would be a sin and a shame. But here come Tom and Billy, if I'm any sort of a guesser."

"Right you are," replied Frank, as he descried two uniformed figures approaching, their heads bent away from the icy gale which was increasing in fury as the night wore on.

"Hello, fellows," was the greeting that came from one of the newcomers, as they came into the flickering light of the street lamp, near which Frank Sheldon and Bart Raymond were standing. "This is a dandy night to be out patrolling—I don't think."

"A good night for ducks, Tom," replied Frank with a laugh.

"For polar bears, if you ask me," put in Billy Waldon, Tom's companion, as he shook the drops from his raincoat. "How would it be to be back in the barracks just now lapping up a smoking hot cup of coffee? Oh, boy!"

"It wouldn't be bad—" Bart was beginning, when suddenly a rifle cracked and a bullet whizzed by so close that it nearly grazed Tom Bradford's ear.

"Shelter, fellows!" shouted Frank, as he leaped for an adjacent hallway.

His companions followed him quickly, and crouching in the hall, they peered out into the darkness to see if they could detect the whereabouts of the would-be assassin.

But everything was quiet except for the roaring of the gale, and the street seemed to be empty.

"Might as well look for a needle in a haystack," muttered Tom Bradford. "We don't even know the direction from which the shot came. You can bet that skunk made tracks as soon as he fired."

"It was a mighty close call for you, Tom," remarked Billy. "A half inch closer and you would have been a goner."

"It would have been hard luck to have been laid out now after having come through that Argonne fighting alive," grumbled Tom. "I'd just like to have my hands right now on the cowardly Heinie who tried to snuff me out."

"Don't you see, Bart, that I was right when I told you that trouble was brewing?" remarked Frank.

"I guess you were, old man."

"It's because we've been too confoundedly easy with these fellows," snorted Billy wrathfully. "We've gone on the theory that if we treated 'em white and gave 'em a square deal they'd appreciate it and behave themselves. We might have known better."

"The French and English know these ginks better than we do, and they've put the boots into them from the start," growled Tom. "There's been no namby-pamby dealing with the Huns in the bridge- heads where they've held control. They've made the Boches walk Spanish. If they didn't uncover when the flag went by, they knocked their hats off for them. They know that the only argument that a Hun understands is force, and they've gone on that theory right along. And as a consequence the Heinies don't dare to peep in the districts where the French and English run things. We ought to take a leaf from their books and do the same."

"That's our good-natured American way of doing things," said Bart. "But we're due to stiffen up a bit now. We're not going to stand for attempts to murder in cold blood—"

He was interrupted by an exclamation from Frank.

"Quiet, fellows," he adjured in a low voice.

"See anything?" whispered Bart, who was nearest him.

"I thought I caught a glimpse of a fellow stealing into that alley half-way down the block," returned Frank. "And there goes another one," he added, with a trace of excitement in his voice.

"I was looking that way and I didn't see anything," murmured Billy Waldon rather incredulously.

"I'd bank on Frank," returned Bart. "He has the best eyes of any of us. They're regular telescopes."

"There goes another!" exclaimed Frank tensely. "There's something doing there, sure as guns!"

"I know that alley," said Tom Bradford. "I've often looked into it when I passed it on my beat. But it's a blind alley and doesn't lead to any thing. It ends at a brick wall."

"All the better chance to bag them," replied Frank. "We'll wait just a minute longer to see If any one else goes in, and then we'll go down and nip the whole bunch. It's against regulations for them to be on the streets at this hour, and you can bet they're up to no good."

"I only hope the fellow's among them that fired that shot," murmured Tom vengefully.

They waited a moment or two longer, but Frank Sheldon's eyes detected no other skulking figure and he gave the word to move.

"Have your clubs and pistols ready, but don't use the guns unless you have to," he ordered, for when the Army Boys were together the leadership by common consent devolved on Frank. "I guess the clubs will do the business if it comes to any resistance on their part."

"Fists would be enough," muttered Tom, as with the others he prepared to follow their leader.

Like so many ghosts they drifted out of the hallway, and, moving in the shadow of the houses, though in the rain and darkness that seemed almost unnecessary, they stealthily approached the entrance to the alley.

It was in one of the poorer sections of the town, and the dwelling houses were interspersed with factories and coal yards. On each side of the alley stood the wall of a factory, three stories in height. No light came from any window, and the alley itself was as dark as pitch.

"Bart and I will stand on this side, and you two fellows take the other side," whispered Frank, when they reached the mouth of the alley. "Keep right on your toes and be ready to nab those fellows when they come out."

The others did as directed and all waited, tense with expectation, their clubs ready for instant service if resistance should be offered.

The rain kept pouring down in torrents, and as it fell, a glaze formed on the sidewalks, so that it was with difficulty that the Army Boys kept their feet.

They were eager to bring the matter to a head, and the waiting in drenching rain wore on their patience.

"Could they have possibly gone out some other way, leaving us here to hold the bag?" queried Bart Raymond, after five minutes had passed without result.

"I don't think so," returned Frank. "I'm dead sure there isn't any way to get out except the way they went in. They're in there holding a pow-wow of some kind."

Ten minutes more passed, and by that time even Frank had begun to have doubts. Tom slipped over to him from the other side of the alley.

"For the love of Mike! let's get a move on and go into the alley and smoke them out," he whispered. "We can get them there just as well as here."

"Just five minutes more," Frank replied. "They may hear us going in and be on their guard, while if we nab them here we'll catch them unawares. But if they're not out in that time, we'll go in and round them up."

At the end of the stipulated time Frank gave the signal.

"Creep in as softly as you can," he admonished his comrades. "Spread across so that they can't slip between us. They've got to be somewhere between us and that brick wall at the back."

Moving with all the caution that their experience as scouts had taught them in their frequent incursions into No Man's Land during the war, the four Army Boys crept noiselessly into the darkness of the alley.

Ten, twenty, thirty feet, and still no sign of their quarry. They must be close to them now.

On they went, wonder gradually giving way to doubt, until with a muttered exclamation Frank came plump up against the wall that marked the alley's end.

"Stung!" he murmured in profound disgust.

His comrades gathered close about him.

"That's one on us," muttered Tom.

"We're done good and proper," agreed Billy.

"Are you dead sure that you saw them come in?" queried Bart of Frank.

"I know I did," replied Frank, who although puzzled was not shaken in his conviction.

"They must have been ghosts then," gibed Tom. "Nothing else could have vanished through a brick wall."

Frank drew his flashlight from his pocket and flashed it about. There was no one to be seen.

"That wall is perfectly blank," he murmured in perplexity. "Thirty feet high if it's an inch. There isn't an opening in it anywhere."

"Could they have got into the windows of the building on either side?" suggested Bart.

Frank swept the flashlight on the walls of the factories.

"Not a chance," he affirmed. "All these windows are protected with iron bars and nothing could get between them. Those fellows seem to have just melted away."

At that instant a report rang out, and the flashlight was knocked from his hand by a bullet.

"Down, fellows!" he shouted, setting the example, and the next moment all four were lying flat on the ground.

They were just in time, for there was a crackling of guns, and other bullets sped over their heads.

"After them, boys!" yelled Frank, leaping to his feet. "They're at the mouth of the alley. I saw the flash from their guns."

He sped for the street with his comrades close upon his heels, their pistols drawn and ready for instant use.

CHAPTER II

WRAPPED IN MYSTERY

The Army Boys looked eagerly about them when they reached the street, but could see no one. It was as though the earth had opened and swallowed the men who had sought their lives.

They scattered and ran in every direction, searching all hallways and side streets for blocks around, but nothing rewarded their endeavors, and it was a bedraggled and exasperated quartette that finally came together again to compare notes and report failure.

"Never saw anything like it in my life!" snorted Tom. "It's as though we were all bewitched. Somebody's wished a jinx on us. Some ghosts are putting up a job on us."

"There was nothing ghostly about that bullet that knocked the flashlight out of my hand or those other bullets that came singing over our heads while we were hugging the ground," said Frank grimly. "If I don't get to the bottom of this, you can call me a Chinaman."

"It gets my goat to think of those Heinies chuckling to themselves because they put one over on us," gritted Billy between his teeth.

"They laugh best who laugh last," growled Bart. "They'll laugh on the other side of their mouth when we lay hands on them."

"If we ever do," muttered pessimistic Tom. "But here comes our relief," he continued, as the light of a lantern hanging on the arm of the foremost man revealed a group coming toward them. "High time, too! I got drenched to the skin while I was lying on the ground in that alley."

"Of course we'll have to report the whole thing to the corporal, shan't we?" inquired Bart.

"I suppose we shall," Frank acquiesced, though reluctantly. "Personally, I'd like to keep the whole thing up my sleeve until we've solved the mystery. But there's danger abroad to-night, and it wouldn't be fair to the boys who are going to take our places not to put them on their guard."

The corporal of the guard now had come so close that the light of his lantern fell upon the group of Army Boys.

"You fellows are all here, I see," said the corporal, who was the boys' old friend, Wilson. "What was that shooting going on here? None of you hurt, I hope."

"Dripping wet but right as a trivet," Frank replied with a smile, and then went on to make his report of the occurrences of the night while the corporal listened with close attention.

"It's certainly strange," he commented when Frank had finished. "It's one of many queer things that are happening lately. I'll report the facts at headquarters and you may be called upon to tell your story there. But now you are off duty, and you can light out for the barracks."

They were only too glad to avail themselves of the permission, and hurried off.

"I've got an idea!" exclaimed Frank, as they scurried along before the gale.

"Frank's got an idea," chaffed Billy. "Hold on to it, old man, for dear life." Frank made a playful pass at him which Billy ducked.

"I've been figuring the thing out," went on Frank, "and I've come to the conclusion that those fellows wanted us to see them go into that alley."

There was an exclamation of surprise from his comrades.

"Come again," said Billy. "I don't get you."

"Why should they want us to see them?" queried Bart. "They might have known that we'd go in after them."

"Sure they did!" answered Frank. "That's just what they wanted. They figured that they'd get us all in there in a bunch. They guessed too that, not finding them, we'd flash a light. That would make us a good target to their confederates who had come to the mouth of the alley, and they thought they could mow us down with one volley. In other words the alley was a trap."

"By ginger, I believe you're right!" exclaimed Bart "The shots came just after the light was flashed. It was a slick trick. You have to hand it to them."

Homer Randall

"But that doesn't explain where the men disappeared to who went into the alley first," remarked Billy.

"No," admitted Frank. "And it doesn't explain either where the men who fired the shots vanished to. But there's an answer to everything, and I'm going to try to find the answer to this. I'm not going to drop it. Of course, I suppose the secret service men will take the thing up, but I'm going to do a little investigating on my own account. I have a hunch that when I take a look at that alley by daylight, I'll tumble to something."

And while the four chums, after their narrow escape, are cudgeling their brains to solve the mystery, it may be well for the sake of those who have not read the preceding volumes of this series to trace briefly their adventures before this story opens.

Frank Sheldon, a vigorous, clean-cut, young fellow, was a resident of Camport, a thriving and prosperous town of about twenty-five thousand people. His father had died a few years before the war broke out, and Frank lived in a little cottage with his mother, of whom for some years he was the sole support. She was of French birth, and by the death of her father had recently come into possession of a considerable estate in France. There had been some legal complications regarding the settlement of the property, and she had intended to go to France to look after her interests when the outbreak of the war made this impossible.

Frank was employed in the wholesale hardware house of Moore and Thomas, and his prospects for the future were very bright when the United States entered the World War. Frank was above everything else a hundred-per-cent American, and if he had consulted only his own wishes would have enlisted at once. But his mother's dependence upon him made him hesitate. An episode occurred, however, that decided him, when he was forced to knock down a burly German who had insulted the American flag. There was no further opposition by his mother, and he joined the Thirty-seventh Regiment, a Camport regiment with a glorious record in the Civil War, and one which had recently seen service on the Mexican border.

Billy Waldon, a close friend of Frank, was already a member, and Bart Raymond, Frank's special chum and a fellow employee, joined also. Another friend, Tom Bradford, tried to join, but was rejected on account of his teeth. He was afterward accepted in the draft, however, so that the four chums, to their great joy, found themselves together in the same regiment.

There was one man in the Moore and Thomas firm who was a bitter and malignant anti-American from the start. His name was Nick Rabig, and he was foreman of one of the departments. He was born in America, but his parents were German. Rabig and Frank Sheldon were at sword's points most of the time because of the former's bullying disposition, and after Rabig had been caught in the draft and forced into the ranks of the old Thirty-seventh he got from Frank the thorough thrashing which had been for a long time coming to him.

What experiences the Army Boys went through in the training camps, how narrowly they escaped a submarine attack on the way to Europe, what exciting adventures they met with on their first contact with the enemy, are described in the first volume of the series entitled: "Army Boys in France; Or, From Training Camp to Trenches."

After they had once reached the scene of action the adventures of the Army Boys multiplied rapidly. Trench warfare was soon outgrown, and open fighting in the field became the order of the day. At one time when the American troops were advancing, the boys became separated from their comrades and were compelled to leap from a broken bridge into a stream, and when they attempted to swim to the other side found themselves in the enemy's hands. For a time a German prison camp with all its horrors loomed up before them, but from this they were saved by a friend of theirs, Dick Lever, who swooped down in his airplane, scattered the enemy guards, and carried his friends back in safety to their own lines.

Frank had the good luck to hear encouraging news about his mother's property from a French colonel whose life he had saved under a rain of fire when the officer, Colonel Pavet, was lying wounded on the battlefield.

Soon, from raw recruits the boys had been developed into skillful soldiers, as is shown in the second volume of the series, entitled: "Army Boys in the French Trenches; Or, Hand to Hand Fights with the Enemy."

The Spring of 1918 had now arrived, and the Germans were preparing for the last desperate drive, on the success of which their fortunes depended. If they could once break through the Allied lines and seize Paris or the Channel ports they would have come near to winning the war, or at any rate, would have greatly delayed the Allies' final victory. The Americans were brought to the front to check the thrust of the Crown Prince's army toward Paris, and the old Thirty-seventh found itself in the very van of the fighting. Tom was captured, and had a series of thrilling experiences before he was able to escape and rejoin his comrades. Nick Rabig came out in his true colors, and his guilt as a traitor was discovered by Tom, while hiding in the woods. How the boys were brought again and again within arm's length of death in the terrific fighting is told in the third volume of the series, entitled: "Army Boys On the Firing Line; Or, Holding Back the German Drive."

On July eighteenth, Marshal Foch struck like a thunderbolt and hurled the foe back in a headlong retreat. Again and again the Germans tried to rally, but the Allies were fired with the certainty of victory and would not be denied.

Frank and his comrades were wherever the fighting was thickest, and did their full share in driving the Germans back to the Rhine. An event which for a time put Frank under a cloud, because it looked as though he were involved in the robbery of a paymaster's clerk, ended in showing that Nick Rabig was the real culprit. This completely vindicated Frank, as will be seen in the fourth volume of the series entitled: "Army Boys In the Big Drive; Or, Smashing Forward to Victory."

That victory was now in sight. The German cause was doomed. One great victory remained to be gained, the clearing of the Argonne forest, wild, tangled, meshed with thousands of miles of barbed wire, crowded with machine gun nests and swept with a hurricane of shot and shell. But nothing could stop America's boys now that their blood was up, and they did much in helping to win here the final and greatest battle of the war. All the Army Boys, fighting like tigers, came through unharmed, except Bart, who was wounded and afterward wandered away from the hospital while temporarily insane.

The armistice was signed and the Army Boys assigned to the Army of Occupation with headquarters at Coblenz. At Luxemburg while on the march they came across an American family who for business reasons had lived for a time in Coblenz. How they took the head of the family for a

German spy, how they marched as conquerors into Germany, how Frank was cheered by learning that his mother's property was sure to come to her, how Bart was found and restored to his right mind, how by the aid of the suspected spy who turned out to be a patriotic American they thwarted a desperate German plot to blow up the fortress of Ehrenbreitstein on the Rhine—all these and other thrilling adventures are described in the fifth volume of the series, entitled: "Army Boys Marching Into Germany; Or, Over the Rhine With the Stars and Stripes".

Since the Army Boys had served as night patrol, they were exempt from getting up when reveille sounded the next morning, and the sun was some hours high when they found themselves together again in their favorite spot in front of the great fortress of Ehrenbreitstein, which formed the principal barracks for the American troops in the occupied zone.

"Well, Mister Detective," said Billy, with a grin, as he slapped Frank on the back, "have you figured out any dope about the fellows who came so near to bumping us off last night?"

"Can't say that I have yet," laughed Frank. "Fact is, I was so dog-tired when I hit the hay last night that I went to sleep the minute my head touched the pillow. And so far this morning I've been so busy packing away grub that I haven't had time to think of anything else. But if I can get leave I'm going over to Coblenz today and take a look at that alley."

"Here comes the corp," remarked Bart, as he saw Wilson approaching. "I wonder whether he found out anything further about last night's rumpus."

"Nothing at all," answered the corporal, who heard the last words. "Everything was quiet for the rest of the night. I stationed two of the men close to the alley with special directions to watch it, but nothing at all happened that was out of the ordinary."

"It's hardly likely that there would," answered Frank. "They wouldn't be likely to try the same game twice in the same night."

"Perhaps they had some special grudge against one or all of you fellows," suggested the corporal. "Have any of you made any special enemies in the town that you know of?"

"I don't think so," replied Frank. "How about it, boys?"

"Not guilty," laughed Billy.

"We've yanked in a few trouble makers from time to time," said Tom thoughtfully, "but we weren't any rougher with them than we had to be."

"I'll tell you!" broke in Bart, as a thought struck him. "It was our bunch that discovered the plot to blow up Ehrenbreitstein and got the tip to our people just in time. Perhaps that's made some of these crazy Huns wild to throw the hooks into us."

"By Jove!" exclaimed Frank, "I never thought of that. I shouldn't wonder if you were more than half right, Bart."

"It may be so," agreed Wilson meditatively. "They certainly were sore when that plot was knocked on the head. They had sworn that no foreign flag should ever float over the greatest fortress in all Germany."

"They swore falsely then," cried Billy jubilantly, as he pointed to the Stars and Stripes floating in the breeze.

Instinctively they took off their caps, as they gazed lovingly upon Old Glory.

CHAPTER III

CAUGHT IN A STORM

"Take a good look at that flag, boys," said the corporal, with a smile, "for it may be some time before you see it again."

"What do you mean?" asked Frank in surprise.

Corporal Wilson smiled at the perplexed and somewhat rueful faces of the four Army Boys.

"Just what I said," he replied to Frank's query. "You fellows are slated to go over the mountain with a bunch of others to round up some of the guns and supplies that the Heinies have promised to surrender. They're slow about it, and have been making all kinds of excuses to keep from bringing them in. The general's patience is just about exhausted, and he's going to get those guns or know the reason why."

"Where is the place?" asked Frank.

"I don't know exactly," answered Wilson. "From the lieutenant who told me to get the boys together for the job I only gathered that it's a good way off. He told me to pick out men that I could rely on, and I thought of you at once. There'll be about fifty of you altogether. You want to get ready to start

Homer Randall

in about two hours."

He passed on to recruit the rest of the detachment, and the boys looked at each other. Frank was thoughtful, Bart indifferent, but Tom and Billy glum.

"Hard luck," growled Tom.

"You said a mouthful!" snorted Billy.

"Look at those boobs," mocked Bart. "I'll bet a dollar to a doughnut that they were planning to go over to see Alice and Helen this afternoon."

  "'Gee whiz, I'm glad I'm free,   No wedding bells for me."

sang Frank.

"Oh, come off!" retorted Tom. "You're simply jealous."

"A perfectly good day gone to waste," grumbled the usually cheerful Billy.

"Cheer up, you hunks of misery," gibed Bart. "The worst is yet to come."

"I'm not specially keen for the trip myself," said Frank. "I'd thought to go over to Coblenz this afternoon and have another look at that place where they so nearly bumped us off last night. But I suppose now that will have to wait."

"The alley will be there when we come back unless there's an earthquake in the meantime," remarked Bart.

"I wish there would be," declared Tom wrathfully. "I'd like to see the whole place wiped off the map. That is," he corrected himself, "if I could get one person out of there before the blow up came."

"Make it two," grinned Billy. "But there's no use grizzling about it. We'll have time anyway to write a letter to the girls telling them all about it. Then, ho! for the mountains and the tricky Huns! I'll be just in the humor to make it hot for them if they don't toe the scratch."

"We'd better get a move on," counseled Frank. "The corp is a hustler, and he'll have that squad together before we know it."

"Hello, what's this?" exclaimed Bart, as they came to a part of the barrack grounds where they caught a glimpse of the road beyond.

Two men were engaged in a heated conversation. One was poorly dressed and had a decided limp, as he tried to keep up with the other, who looked like a professional man of some kind. The former was evidently pleading with the latter, who shook off impatiently the hand that had been placed on his arm.

"Scrapping about something," remarked Tom carelessly.

The lame man still persisted, and suddenly his companion swung around and aimed a blow at him with his cane. The other dodged and the cane was lifted again, but before it could fall, Frank had reached the man's side and wrenched the cane from his hand.

The owner turned with a glare of fury, which changed however to a look of apprehension as his eyes fell on the American uniform.

He mumbled something that might have been an apology or an explanation, but Frank cut him short.

"Hitting a lame man doesn't go around here," said Frank curtly. "If you had actually hit him, I'd have done the same thing to you."

The man was cowed and made no reply. The lame man meanwhile had hobbled away. Frank handed back the cane, turned his back upon the owner and rejoined his companions.

"True Prussian brutality," commented Bart. "Good work, old boy. But now let's hurry or we'll be late."

They scattered to their quarters, and in a short time were fully equipped for the coming journey.

When a little later they had assembled at the place the corporal had appointed, they found there a group of their comrades selected from the old Thirty-seventh bent on the same errand as themselves. Lieutenant Winter was in command of the detachment, which numbered about half a hundred.

"Mighty good name for the leader of this trip," Bart whispered jokingly to Frank, as they stood drawn up in line awaiting the command to start.

"It certainly is," agreed Frank, drawing his coat a little closer. "This is about as bitter weather as I've ever stacked up against."

"Looks to me as if a snow storm were coming," murmured Billy.

"Attention!" came the sharp command. "Forward, march!"

The lines moved forward as one man, the lieutenant riding ahead on horseback and two motor trucks loaded with supplies bringing up the rear.

The road led at first along the bank of the river and was fairly level. After two miles had been traversed the line of march swerved sharply toward the right and the men began to climb.

The weather was biting cold, and a stinging-wind whipped their cheeks and searched their clothing. But they were warmly clad and the pace at which they marched kept them comfortable enough. Their sturdy frames were inured to hardships, and they joked and laughed as they went along.

Soon they had passed through the little suburban villages that hung on the flank of Coblenz, and the way was interspersed with farmhouses at longer and longer intervals. The country became wilder, and as the path wound upward, they soon found themselves in the midst of mountains, on the other side of which lay the town for which they were bound.

The leafless branches of great trees waved creakily over their heads as the wind whistled through them. There was no sign of human life or habitation to, be seen. For all that appeared to the contrary, they might have been in the depths of a primeval forest.

"The jumping off place," muttered Tom, as at the command of the lieutenant the detachment paused for a short rest.

"The little end of nowhere, I'll tell the world," returned Billy, gazing about him. "Gee, what a place to be lost in!"

There was only a brief time permitted for rest, as the lieutenant was anxious to get his men over the ridge and at their destination before the short winter afternoon came to an end. The men fell in and the march went on.

The sky had now become a steely gray, and flakes of snow began to fall. They came down slowly at first and then more rapidly, and the ground was soon covered. The wind too had increased in intensity, and the boys soon found themselves in what promised to develop into a genuine blizzard.

The road had dwindled now to a mere mountain path, and even this was soon obliterated by the snow that was becoming deeper every minute.

Suddenly Bart tripped over a root and fell full-length on the snow. He tried to rise, but could not bear his weight upon his foot, which gave way under him. His comrades, who had laughed at first, sprang to help him. They drew him to one side, while Wilson came to see what the matter was.

"It's nothing," explained Bart, as he stood with an arm flung over the shoulders of Tom and Billy, while Frank, on his knees, vigorously rubbed and manipulated his ankle. "I'll be all right in a minute. It was a boob stunt for me to do."

"Nothing broken?" inquired Wilson anxiously.

"No," answered Frank, looking up but keeping on with his rubbing. "I can feel that the foot's all right. He's just strained it a little, that's all."

"Good," said Wilson. "You fellows come on after us then as soon as you can," and he hurried back to his place.

Two or three minutes more and Bart was able to walk, although he limped a trifle. They picked up their rifles and hurried after their comrades.

In the gathering dusk they did not notice that a trail diverged from the main one that they had been traveling, and they turned into this side trail, straining their eyes through the whirling snow to catch a glimpse of their comrades.

They had gone on for about ten minutes, not talking in order to save their breath, when Frank put into words the growing uneasiness of all of them.

"Queer that we haven't caught up to them yet!" he exclaimed, peering ahead, although he could not see more than twenty paces through the blinding snow.

"We certainly are traveling a good deal faster than they were when we saw them last," declared Bart.

"They must have got hold of some seven-league boots," grumbled Tom.

"Put on a little more speed," advised Billy. "Make it snappy now, and we're bound to catch up with them."

They quickened their pace, but without result. There were no footprints to be seen, but that meant nothing, for the snow covered up all tracks almost as soon as they were made.

For twenty minutes more they hurried along as well as they could through the snow that clogged and clung to their feet, and at last the truth forced itself upon their unwilling minds.

"No use, fellows," said Frank, as he stopped and the others gathered around him. "There's no use kidding ourselves any longer. We might as well own up to it that we've taken the wrong trail."

"Guess you're right, old man," said Tom disconsolately. "It

Homer Randall

simply wouldn't be possible for us not to have caught up to them at the rate we've been going. We're up against it for fair, and the question is, how we're going to get out of it. Getting snowbound in this wilderness doesn't make any hit with me."

"There's only one thing to do," said Frank decidedly, "and that is to right about face and try to find the place where we turned off."

"Swell chance," muttered Tom. "It's getting dark now by the minute, and it'll be as black as pitch in a little while."

"I know it's a forlorn hope," admitted Frank, "but it's the only thing to do just the same, and even forlorn hopes have a way of winning out sometimes. We can't stand here and be frozen to death. Perhaps we'll find some of the fellows sent back to look for us. Get a hustle on now."

He set the pace, and they followed with a speed that under other conditions they would not have thought possible.

But fast as they went, the snow and the darkness came faster, and despite all their efforts they were not able to find where the paths diverged. Everywhere was one bleak wilderness of snow. Soon they had all lost the path they were following and found themselves floundering through the woods among the tree trunks. There was no use in going further, for in the dense darkness they were quite as likely to be going away from their comrades as toward them, and at last Frank called a halt.

"The storm's got us, fellows," he declared, with a forced laugh that had little mirth in it.

"All my fault," remarked Bart gloomily. "I guess I'm a Jonah,

I picked out the wrong moment to take a tumble. Now we're in a fine mess."

"We've been in worse," said Billy cheerily, "and pulled through them just the same."

"That's the way to talk!" exclaimed Frank heartily, giving Billy a slap on the back. "We'll get out of this scrape as we have out of a lot of others. At the worst, it's only a matter of having to wait till daylight. We're worth a dozen dead men yet. At any rate we've got grub with us, so that there's no danger of our starving."

"How about freezing to death?" said Tom, who was always inclined to see the dark side of things.

"We won't do that either," replied Frank. "That is, if we keep moving, and that's what we've got to do. It may not get us anywhere, but at least it will keep the blood circulating. Then too, there's the odd chance of our stumbling upon some hut or other where we can find some kind of shelter."

"Better let me go first, then," put in Bart. "I'm good at stumbling. In fact it's my long suit."

They all laughed and felt better.

"We don't know where we're going, but we're on the way," sang out Billy, as they began to trudge forward.

They had plenty of rations with them, and they munched some food as they went along. It was cold comfort, but it was comfort just the same.

"Oh, you hot coffee!" murmured Billy, and at the picture that he conjured up the others groaned.

The snow was now knee deep and showed no signs of letting up, though the wind had abated somewhat in violence.

They plodded on through the heavy drifts that clutched at their tired legs like so many nightmare hands trying to hold them back to their destruction. They were young and hardy, but their physical strength was sorely tested by the battle with the elements. Their hearts were thumping as though they would burst through their ribs, and their breath came in gasps.

Suddenly Frank's keen eyes caught sight of a dark mass that seemed to stand out even blacker than the darkness which was everywhere around them. He rubbed his eyes clear of the snow that clung to the lashes and looked again. Then he gave a shout.

"We've found it, boys!" he yelled. "There's a building of some kind just ahead of us. See it? See it?"

They looked and saw, and with a joyful shout make a break for shelter.

CHAPTER IV

THE RUINED CASTLE

As the Army Boys drew closer, the building seemed to grow in size. Wing after wing detached itself from the mass that seemed to cover fully an acre of ground. There were no fences to hinder their approach, but there were great masses of broken blocks and masonry through which they had to wind their way before they found themselves before a frowning tower, whose peak rose above the top of a quadrangular group of buildings surrounding it.

"Why, it's an old castle of some kind!" exclaimed Frank, as they paused at the foot of the tower, spent and breathless.

"I don't care what it is," replied Bart. "It's shelter of some kind, and that's enough for me."

"Wonder if there's any one living here," remarked Billy Waldon, his eyes sweeping the great mass for some sign of life. "Even the bark of a dog would be welcome to-night."

"Not a light anywhere," commented Tom. "If there's anybody living here I guess they're dead."

"There's not even a door to knock at," said Frank Sheldon,

looking into the yawning space of what had evidently been an entrance to the tower. "I guess we'll have to go on a little exploring expedition. Come along, fellows, and get out of the wind. Lucky that I have my flashlight along."

They crowded in on their leader's heels, first, as a precaution, seeing that their weapons were ready, though there did not seem to be the faintest chance of their being required.

Frank drew his flashlight, and the streaming rays illuminated a long passageway whose end they could not see. There were open spaces in the roof and walls through which the snow had drifted in spots, but there were other parts that were clear and dry, and these were welcomed by the boys with immense relief after their long battle with the snow.

At a turning of the corridor they came upon a large room that, although mildewed and dilapidated and wholly bereft of furniture, was intact as far as the walls and ceiling were concerned. But what especially caught their eyes was a huge stone fireplace, and at once they decided to end their explorations for the present right there.

"Perhaps that hot coffee wasn't such a dream after all," chuckled Billy. "We've got plenty of the stuff in our kits, and all we need is some hot water."

"There's no end of broken branches about here," said Frank. "Let's get a pile of them in here, and we'll have a fire started in less than no time."

Though Tom said that the wood would probably be too wet to burn, he turned in heartily with the others, and in a few minutes they had a bigger pile of wood ready than probably the old room had ever seen before. Then by careful nursing of some chips and twigs a blaze was started that soon developed into a roaring fire, before which the boys stood and dried out their wet clothes and toasted themselves until they were in a glow.

The coffee problem was now a simple one, as all they had to do was to melt snow enough to furnish the hot water, and they used the cooking utensils that they had in their kits, for they had started out that afternoon in full marching order. Savory odors soon announced that the fragrant brew was ready, and they almost scalded their throats in the eagerness to partake of it.

"Yum-yum!" murmured Tom after his second cup. "Nectar has nothing on this."

"I'll say so," agreed Billy, with a blissful expression on his face.

"We never knew how good it was until we thought we couldn't get it," grinned Bart.

"Maybe this isn't a contrast to things as they were an hour ago, eh, fellows?" laughed Frank. "Listen to the wind screaming round this building, mad because it can't get at us."

"I wonder what the rest of the bunch are thinking about us just now," remarked Billy.

"I suppose they're worried to death, because we didn't turn up," replied Frank. "They've probably got squads out hunting for us at this minute. They've probably guessed what happened when we failed to catch up with them."

"Well, there isn't a chance in a thousand of their striking this place," said Tom, yawning. "In the meantime, I'm all tired out and vote that we hit the hay."

"There isn't any hay to hit, worse luck," said Bart, looking about him ruefully. "It's the stone floor for us to-night, all right. But it's warm and dry, and we'll make out with our blankets. It'll beat traveling around in the snow all night, any way."

"Let's get some more wood so that we'll have enough to last all night," suggested Frank, and followed by the others he suited the action to the word.

"How about some of us standing watch?" remarked Bart, when the huge pile of branches had been heaped within easy distance of the fire.

"Don't see any need of it," remarked Tom, rubbing his eyes. "We're probably miles away from any living thing and there's nothing to watch for except ghosts. There ought to be plenty of those around in a place so old as this. But who wants to watch for ghosts? I'd rather be asleep than awake if any of those old codgers come perambulating around."

"Quit your kidding," replied Frank with a laugh. "But I think we ought to stand watch, turn and turn about. There's a bare chance that some of the detachment may come this way, though I don't think it's likely. Then again we're really in an enemy's country, and it wouldn't be good soldiering for all of us to go to sleep. Besides, the fire has got to be kept up."

They felt the force of this and agreed.

"Let's see," remarked Frank, as he consulted his radio watch, "I figure it will be about eight hours till daylight. That'll be two hours for each of us."

"You fellows go to sleep," broke in Bart, "and I'll stand watch all night. That's only right, for I'm the fellow who got you into this fix."

"Nonsense!" said Frank. "That doesn't go with this bunch. We'll share and share alike, or else there's nothing doing."

Bart still persisted, but the others overruled him and he had to give in.

Frank drew a memorandum book from his pocket, tore out a page and made four strips of different lengths. The one that drew the shortest was to stand the first watch and the others were to take their turn according to the length of their strips. Bart drew the shortest, and Billy, Tom, and Frank followed, the latter having the longest slip remaining in his hand.

"If you go to sleep, Bart, you'll be shot at sunrise," joked Billy.

"I'm all right then," retorted Bart, "for I never get up that early."

Frank, Billy, and Tom spread their blankets as near the fire as was safe, and rolled themselves in them. The bed was hard, but this bothered them little, and they were so tired that they were asleep almost as soon as they stretched themselves out.

Bart, too, was more exhausted than he ever remembered being in all his life before, and from time to time he looked enviously at the forms of his sleeping comrades. The two hours that stretched before him would be very long ones.

At times he would pace slowly about the room, stopping now and then to replenish the fire. His foot still hurt him a little, and he frequently sat down in a corner to rest himself. He found, however, that this was dangerous, for an almost uncontrollable drowsiness would steal over him, despite all his efforts to keep awake. The only way he could feel sure of staying awake was to keep on his feet.

An hour passed and half of another.

He was counting the minutes now before he would be relieved, when suddenly, as he was passing the entrance that opened on the corridor, he heard a sound that startled him.

He stood stock still, every trace of sleepiness gone in an instant and all his faculties keenly on the alert. But nothing happened and he relaxed.

"Pshaw!" he said to himself impatiently. "What's the matter with me? Am I letting what Tom said about ghosts get on my nerves?"

Then the sound came again, and this time Bart knew that he was not mistaken.

CHAPTER V

CONSPIRATORS

What Bart heard was the sound of human voices.

At first the thought flashed across him that they might be those of some of his comrades, sent back by Lieutenant Winter to look for the missing men.

But he dismissed this thought almost as soon as it was formed. There was a peculiar quality about the tones that was not American, a coarse guttural sound such as he had grown only too familiar with in the streets of Coblenz. Those who were talking were Germans.

He listened intently.

It was evident from the varying tones that there were quite a number of men in the group. At times the conversation seemed animated, and then again there would be a lull. Once he thought he heard them quarreling.

What could these men be doing here in the dead of night? Was it possible that some part of the castle was inhabited after all? Or had they gathered together for some secret and lawless purpose?

Bart thought at first that he would wake his companions and tell them what he had heard. On second thought, however, he concluded that he would do a little reconnoitering on his own account. They were so utterly tired that he hated to wake them for what after all might prove to be not worth while.

Carefully looking to his weapons, he stole from the room and moved in the direction of the voices.

But this was not so easy a matter as he thought. The old castle proved to be a perfect maze of rooms, some connected and others detached, and again and again he found himself going further away from the sounds and having to retrace his steps. Then too he was afraid to flash a light, and had to grope his way over the uneven floor and amid piles of debris.

At last, however, he found himself on the right track. A faint ray of light from a distant room gave him the clue. Moving with the stealth of an Indian on the trail, he crept forward until at the end of a distant corridor he found what he sought.

In a large room, lighted by a fire that blazed on the hearth and by three or four candles, were a number of men engaged in animated conversation. A glance at their features showed that all were Germans. Some of the men were in civilian clothes, but others wore old, dilapidated army uniforms.

They were a rough looking lot, and Bart saw at a glance that most of them were armed. They were gathered about a man with a red, bushy beard, who seemed to be the leader. He had a map spread on a table improvised from boxes, and was pointing out places indicated by red dots.

Bart counted the men. There were nine burly fellows, who looked desperate and as though they could give a good account of themselves in rough and tumble work. In one of the guns standing against the wall Bart noted a red flag thrust in the muzzle—the symbol of the German revolutionary element that was spreading terror throughout the former empire.

He could hear distinctly now what the speakers said, but his knowledge of German was limited and he could not get the full meaning. He heard repeatedly however the words "Coblenz," "Liebknecht," and "Spartacide." He knew what was meant by those baleful words. They meant the over-throw of law and order, a program of blood and massacre. And they were discussing this program evidently with reference to Coblenz, where the American Army of Occupation had its headquarters.

Bart pondered what he should do. It was out of the question for him alone to attack these conspirators. They were too many for any single man. He must arouse his comrades at once.

With the utmost caution he tiptoed back, and finding the room, not without some difficulty, bent over the sleepers. They were dead with sleep and he had to shake them to get them wide awake, but the news he whispered to them had them on edge and ready for action in an instant.

They crowded together for a whispered conference.

"What would we better do?" asked Billy.

"There's just one thing to do," said Frank, "and that is to nab the whole bunch. That is," he went on, "if we find that they're really hatching mischief, as Bart thinks. I've picked up enough German in the last few months to be able to understand what they're talking about, and on a pinch I could even talk with them after we've got them under our guns."

"But are you sure we have any right to arrest them?" asked Bart, a little doubtfully.

"Sure we have," answered Frank promptly. "You said they were armed, didn't you?"

"Yes," replied Bart.

"That's all the excuse we need then to nip this thing in the bud," Frank answered. "It's against regulations for the Germans to carry arms in the zone occupied by the American army, and any one who does is liable to arrest on sight. See that your guns are all right, fellows, and come along. I have a hunch that we're going to give these plotters a surprise party. But we'll listen first and make sure before we pinch them."

Bart went in advance to show the way, and his comrades crept after him, drifting along like so many ghosts.

The conference was still in progress, but it had somewhat changed its character. When Bart had been listening, it had been a debate in which all were taking more or less part. Now the man with the red beard was making a speech. He had taken the red flag from the gun muzzle and waved it from time to time to punctuate his remarks. He had worked himself up into a passion as he progressed. His eyes were bulging, his face inflamed, as he poured out a torrent of words that evidently carried away his hearers, to judge from their rapt attention and the frequent ejaculations that burst from them.

The Army Boys listened for several minutes, and then at a sign from Frank drew back a little distance, while he spoke to them in whispers.

"It's what I thought," he murmured. "That fellow is an

agitator from Berlin who has come to stir up trouble in the Coblenz district. He's urging these men to start an uprising that will take the American troops by surprise and wipe them out. From something he said I have an idea that he was concerned in the plot to blow up Ehrenbreitstein. He's as dangerous as a rattlesnake, and we've got to get him.

"Now," he went on, "just back me up when I give the word. They're nine to our four, but we have the advantage of surprise. Follow my lead and we'll bag them all right."

CHAPTER VI

THE BAFFLED PLOTTERS

When the Army Boys got back to the room the orator was winding up his speech. He finished with an eloquent peroration, and his hearers broke into applause as the last word left his lips.

Frank leaped into the room with his rifle leveled directly at the leader.

"Hands up!" he shouted.

At the same instant, the rest of the Army Boys followed their leader, their rifles sweeping the room.

The effect of the sudden entrance of the Army Boys was electric.

With a roar of rage and chagrin, the conspirators made as though they would rush on the intruders. But the wicked looking muzzles of the army rifles and the look of determination in the faces of the boys who held them produced a change.

Slowly the hands went up until all were raised above

their heads.

"Hold them there now," commanded Frank. "The first one who moves is a dead man."

Most of them could not understand the words, but as they looked into Frank's eyes they had not the slightest doubt of his meaning, and they stood like so many statues, only their eyes and the working of their features betraying the impotent anger that possessed them.

"Now, Tom," said Frank, without removing his eyes from those of the German leader, "go over these men and take whatever weapons they may have, while the rest of you keep the bunch covered."

Tom laid aside his rifle and did the work with promptness and thoroughness, and his search was rewarded by a considerable collection of knives and pistols. To these he added the rifles that had been leaning against the wall, and removed the lot from the room.

"They haven't anything left more dangerous than a toothpick," he reported to Frank, with a grin, as he picked up his rifle and resumed his place.

"Fine and dandy," remarked Frank.

"Now," he went on, addressing the prisoners, "back up to that wall and sit down on the floor. Quick now! *Sitzen Sie sich. Verstehen Sie?"*

They understood, and showed that they did by obeying, though if looks could kill Frank would have been blasted by the venomous glance that the German leader shot at him.

Only then did Frank permit himself to relax. He lowered his rifle with a sense of relief.

"We've got them corralled now," he remarked to his comrades. "Let your rifles down, boys, but keep your eyes on them. If any one of them tries to make a break, we can pot him before he gets to his feet."

"Well, now that we've got them what are we going to do with them?" asked Billy.

"Sort of white elephant on our hands it seems to me," said Tom, in some perplexity.

"No more sleep for any of us to-night, I guess," observed Bart.

"Oh, I don't know," said Frank. "Two of us will be enough to guard these fellows at a time, while the others get a few winks. I think I'll question the fellow who seems to be running this shooting match and see if I can get anything out of him."

He motioned to the leader to get to his feet and come forward, which the latter did with a thunderous frown on his face.

Frank had a faint hope that the man would be able to speak English, in which case his task would be comparatively easy. But when he asked the captive in German whether he could speak English, the latter replied with a surly negative.

So Frank was compelled to muster his limited vocabulary and pick out enough German to make himself understood. In that language, then, the questioning proceeded.

"What were you men doing here?" asked Frank.

"By what authority do you ask me?" the prisoner responded. "Since when has it been a crime for Germans to meet together on German soil?"

"That depends on the purpose of the meeting," answered Frank. "You may be on German soil, but just now you are under American laws, and they don't allow such meetings unless permission is received in advance. Besides, Germans are forbidden to have arms. How about those weapons we've just taken away from you?"

"If there are any laws like that they ought to be broken," replied the prisoner impudently.

"Don't get gay with me now," said Frank, with an ominous glitter in his eyes. "We taught your armies a lesson not long ago, and you'll find that we can teach you civilians just as easily."

"Our armies were not beaten," the man answered with a sudden flare of rage. "They could have fought for years if it had not been for the hunger at home."

"They gave a pretty good imitation of beaten armies then," said Frank sarcastically, "and I had an idea that the Americans had something to do with the beating. But that's neither here nor there. What were you planning to do at Coblenz?"

"Nothing," growled the prisoner.

"That doesn't go with me," replied Frank. "I happened to hear some of that speech of yours and Coblenz was sprinkled through it rather thickly. Suppose you hand over to me that map with the red dots marked on it."

"I have no map," the man replied, a look of apprehension coming into his eyes.

"Lying again, are you?" said Frank. "Bart, cover this fellow with your rifle while Billy goes through his pockets."

The prisoner's fist clenched, but a prod of Bart's rifle made him think better of it, and Billy drew from one of the inside pockets of the man's coat the identical map over which the group had been poring when Bart first came upon the scene.

"That'll do," said Frank. "Go back to the wall and sit down. Your case will be attended to by the American authorities at Coblenz."

The German, with a muttered imprecation, did as he was told, and while Bart kept his eye on the group of prisoners, Frank and the other Army Boys looked over the map.

They had been so long in Coblenz that they knew the town from end to end, and could readily identify the places that on the map were splashed with red. They included all the places occupied as headquarters by staffs of the various brigades and divisions of the American Army, as well as the American hospital and other buildings devoted to army uses.

"What do the red marks mean, do you think?" asked Billy, with lively curiosity.

"Blood or bombs or something of that kind, I suppose," replied Frank. "Taking this with what I gathered from the fellow's speech, I think it marks places that are to be blown up. It looks like a general uprising against American rule. I think that Army headquarters will find this little sheet of paper an interesting thing to study. And it wouldn't surprise me very much if our genial friend over there should find himself before long standing before a firing squad."

"What is this place here?" asked Tom, putting his finger on one of the red spots.

"I don't know of any government building there," commented Billy. Frank took another look.

"Why, fellows," he said with quickening interest, "that's where the alley is that we were so nearly trapped in the other night. Don't you recognize it?"

"Sure enough," agreed Billy. "But what is there that they would want to blow up?"

"Maybe some of these red spots are meant to indicate meeting places of the conspirators," suggested Frank. "See, there's a little red cross added here that you don't find in connection with the army and government buildings. But it's queer that that alley should turn up again. I wish I knew what it meant."

"Well, we'll have to let the Secret Service ferret that out," said Billy. "They have fellows there to whom this will be as clear as crystal after they've studied it a little. In the meantime we've got a big enough job on our hands to take care of these prisoners. What are we going to do with them?"

"We've got time to think that over between now and daylight," answered Frank. "For the present we'll make them lie down flat and far enough apart so that they can't talk with each other. Then you and I will stand the first watch and Bart and Tom the next. As soon as daylight comes we must be on the move."

The plan was carried out, although Bart and Tom declared that they had lost all desire for sleep and would keep awake with the others. Frank, however, wanted to have them in good shape when morning came, and the plan was carried out. As a matter of fact, Bart and Tom were fast asleep in five minutes, and Frank and Billy yielded as readily when their turn came.

With the first streak of dawn, the boys were on their feet.

"Doped it out yet?" Bart asked of Frank.

"Pretty well," his chum answered. "I've figured out that we'd do better to try to find our detachment than to go back with these fellows to Coblenz. In the first place, it must be nearer, and then, too, we have the chance of meeting some of the detachment who have probably been sent out to look for us. The sun will give us the general direction and we'll probably hit the camp before long."

"Perhaps some of the prisoners could give us the direction," suggested Bart.

"I suppose most any of them could," answered Frank. "Some of them, no doubt, are natives of this section, though that big red beard comes from Berlin. But do you think I'd trust any of them? Not on your life! They'd only lead us into a trap."

"I guess you're right," agreed Bart.

"How about breakfast for these Huns?" asked Tom.

"We'll have to rustle some grub for them, of course," answered Frank. "Haven't they got any food with them?"

"A few hunks of bread and cheese," answered Tom, "but not

nearly enough to go around. We'll have to give them some of our rations, I suppose, though we made quite a hole in them last night and there isn't very much left."

"Well, we'll divide up with them as long as we have any," said Frank, "though I know mighty well they wouldn't do it with us if the case were reversed."

"You bet they wouldn't," answered Tom, "I've been a prisoner in their hands, and I know what I'm talking about."

They made coffee and distributed food, giving to their prisoners as much as they ate themselves. Then Frank lined up the prisoners and directed them to go ahead in the general direction he pointed out, warning them sternly that he would not hesitate to shoot at the least sign of resistance or any attempt to escape.

The storm had ceased, although a bitter wind was still blowing and heaping the snow in drifts. Still this had some advantages, for while it piled the snow deep in places it swept other spots almost clean and they made fairly rapid progress. The prisoners marched sulkily but steadily, with a wholesome respect for the rifles behind them and the men who held them.

They had been marching for perhaps an hour through the bleak forest, when Bart gave a sudden exclamation.

"See those black dots on the snow?" he said, pointing ahead and a little to the right. "They're moving and they're coming this way! I'll bet it's some of our fellows sent out to find us."

Frank looked hard and long, and as he looked his face grew grave. He did not seem to share his comrade's jubilation.

"Guess again, Bart," he said.

"Why?" asked Bart.

"Because," replied Frank, "those fellows are wearing German uniforms. They're probably a lot of disbanded soldiers on their way home. I rather think, boys, that we're in for a fight."

CHAPTER VII

A CLOSE CALL

There was a stir among the Army Boys as they crowded around their leader.

"Are you sure, Frank?" asked Billy.

"Positive," answered Frank. "I can tell by their uniform and by their walk. I could even make out that some of them were wearing the uniform of the Jaeger regiments. They fought against us in the Argonne, and you'll remember that they're pretty tough birds. If it comes to a scrap we'll have our work cut out for us."

"But why should there be any scrap?" questioned Tom. "Germans are arrested every day in Coblenz and no one tries to rescue them."

"That's different," replied Frank. "The people know there that we've got powerful forces right at hand that could crush any attempt at rescue. But that doesn't count much out in the wilderness. If these fellows have an officer with them, he'll probably have sense enough to know that it doesn't pay to buck up against the United States army. But if they're just traveling along without organization, they feel so sore at us that they may be willing to take a chance and mix in."

"How many do you make them out to be?" asked Billy.

"About fifteen, I should judge," was the answer.

"What are you going to do?" asked Bart.

"Keep right ahead in the direction we are going. The boldest way is usually the best. If they saw us do any pussyfooting, they'd think we were scared, and they'd come after us anyway."

The two parties were not traveling in such a line that they would necessarily meet each other. Under ordinary conditions they would have passed at a distance of perhaps six hundred feet. But as the other party approached, Frank could see that one of their number was observing him and his comrades through a pair of field glasses. There was a hurried consultation, and then the newcomers swerved from their line of march and came directly toward the Army Boys.

"Just what I expected," muttered Frank, as his eyes darted from place to place over the snowy landscape to find a favorable position from a military point of view.

A hundred feet away was a slight rise of ground from which grew a clump of gigantic oak trees. They were so close together that their roots seemed to intermingle. On the near side of the little hill the vagaries of the wind had swept the snow into a sort of cave formation, leaving a space in the center hollowed out with great banks of snow on both sides.

Straight into this cave-like space Frank marched his group of prisoners who were walking with their hands upraised, but resting on their heads so as to ease their arms.

"You stand here, Billy, with your gun leveled, and if any one of these fellows makes a break drop him in his tracks," Frank directed, "You, Bart and Tom, come with me, and we'll go ahead and have a parley with this gang, and see what their intentions are."

The newcomers had now approached within a distance of a hundred yards. The boys looked in vain for any one wearing an officer's uniform, but there was no one who seemed to be in command. The crowd advanced in straggling formation, some of their faces exhibiting merely curiosity, while those of others were ugly and determined. There were perhaps half a dozen rifles among the lot, but the boys could see army revolvers at the belts of half a dozen more. A few had nothing but heavy sticks. The clothing of all was worn and travel stained, but all were of military cut and pattern, indicating that the wearers had belonged to the German army. The Army Boys went boldly toward them, and their confident bearing seemed to impress the Germans, who hesitated in their advance and crowded close together as though in consultation.

The boys kept going until they were within thirty feet, and then Frank handed his rifle to Billy and went forward with empty hands to show that his intentions were peaceable.

"We're American soldiers, as you can see by our uniforms," he said in a clear voice, in which there was no trace of wavering. "We are on our way to camp. We saw you turn from your line of march and come our way as though you wanted to speak to us. What do you want?"

Frank had spoken in German and they all understood him, but there was no answer ready, although the men's eyes glowered as they rested on his uniform and there were muttered exclamations.

"Is there any one of you that speaks English?" Frank asked, after waiting a moment.

Again a whispered consultation, and one of their number was pushed forward by the others.

"Do you speak English?" Frank asked.

"Yes," replied the man roughly. "I lived for five years in your accursed America."

The tone and words were offensively insolent, but Frank took no notice of them.

"Then perhaps you can tell me what you and your comrades want with us," he said.

"We want those prisoners you have with you," the man replied.

"What prisoners?" parried Frank.

"Don't try to fool us," the man answered angrily. "We saw those men walking with their hands on their heads, and we know they are Germans. We want them, and we're going to have them."

"How are you going to get them?" Frank asked quietly.

"How are we going to get them?" sneered the man. "Why, by taking them, if we have to. There are only four of you, as we saw through our glasses, and we're four to one. You wouldn't be fools enough to fight against such odds. If you give them up peaceably we won't hurt you. But if you don't, we'll wipe you out."

"Now listen," said Frank sternly. "We've arrested these men because they were plotting against the United States. We've set out to take them into camp, and we're going to do it. This district is under American rule and America has a long arm. You may wipe us out, but the American Government will reach out that arm and get you, no matter where you try to hide. I warn you to go on your way and let us pass."

"It's fight then, is it?" snarled the German.

He turned to his companions.

"Comrades!" he roared.

But he got no further.

Like lightning, Frank's left hand shot out and gripped the man by the collar. With his right, he yanked his automatic pistol from his belt and clapped it against the man's temple.

"One move and I'll blow your brains out," he snapped.

The man, after his first instinct of revolt, stood like a statue. That cold muzzle against his head was a compelling argument.

There was a wild commotion among the Germans, and rifles were raised, but as Frank had whirled his prisoner between him and them they did not dare to fire, but stood raging but irresolute.

Walking backward with his prisoner, the pistol still pressed to his head, Frank rejoined Bart and Tom, whose rifles were leveled at the crowd. Step by step the boys retreated, until they stood with Billy in the shelter of the oaks. Frank then delivered his prisoner to Billy, who made him lie down in the snow cave with the others.

"Good work, old man!" said Tom admiringly, as he clapped Frank on the shoulder.

"I'll tell the world so," agreed Bart enthusiastically.

"Gee, but my heart was in my mouth while I watched you," said Billy.

"Have any trouble with the prisoners while I was gone?" asked Frank.

"Not much," grinned Billy. "Redbeard tried to get up, but I handed him a clip on the jaw and he sat down again."

"Drop!" shouted Bart suddenly. "Those fellows are getting ready to fire."

They threw themselves flat on the snow, and a moment later some bullets zipped over them.

"Looks as though they meant business," muttered Frank.

"Lucky that they haven't all got rifles," remarked Billy.

"Seems like the old Argonne days come again, only on a smaller scale," remarked Tom. "Shall we let them have a taste of lead, Frank? My finger's fairly itching to pull the trigger."

"Hold in a while, Tom," counseled Frank. "They have done that to vent their spite. We're safe enough behind these oaks, and we haven't any too much ammunition. If they show any signs of making a rush, we'll let them have a volley."

"That's just what they're going to do," remarked Bart. "They know they're four to one and they're going to take a chance."

"Five to one, really," answered Frank, "for Billy will have his hands full in guarding the prisoners."

Another volley came at that minute, and several bullets embedded themselves in the oaks. At the same moment, the Germans rushed forward a few yards, taking shelter behind what trees they could or throwing themselves behind hillocks of snow.

"They're in earnest," remarked Tom.

"All right," said Frank, and his fingers tightened on his rifle. "Let them rush us. They'll get all that's coming to them."

CHAPTER VIII

JUST IN TIME

"Those fellows are old campaigners," commented Bart. "You can tell that by the tactics they're using. It's the old system they tried at the Marne and in the Argonne, making a rush for a few yards, throwing themselves flat, and then repeating the process until they got near enough to rush us."

"A pretty good system, too," commented Tom, "but it didn't win then and it isn't going to win now. Just watch me wing one or two of these Huns and put a crimp into their tactics."

His chance came even while he was speaking, for one of the Germans thrust his rifle out from behind a tree and fired. At the same instant, Tom's rifle cracked, and the bullet ploughed its way through the man's right shoulder. He fell with a groan and rolled out from behind his shelter on to the snow. He was an easy mark as he lay there, but Tom refrained from firing again. The man was out of the fight and as good as dead as far as any further offensive was concerned. Besides, it was no part of the American idea of war to kill a wounded foe, although it was a matter of record that it had frequently been done by the Germans.

"Good shooting, old man," commented Frank. "You haven't

got out of the way of potting them."

"One less to cause us trouble," remarked Billy. "Gee, if I didn't have these prisoners to watch! I'm getting cross-eyed, trying to keep one eye on them and the other on these fellows that are trying to rush us."

"Keep both eyes on the prisoners," directed Frank, "especially on that red-beard person. He's bad medicine. We'll handle these fellows. Ah, you will, will you?"

The last exclamation was prompted by one of the Germans who tried at that moment to glide from a small tree behind which he was sheltered to a larger one that seemed to promise better protection. He moved swiftly, but Frank's bullet was swifter, and the man went down with a bullet in his thigh.

"Talk about sniping," grinned Bart. "Those fellows will wake up after a while to the fact that they've tackled a hornet's nest. Even a thick German head can take in an idea sometimes."

"Especially if it's pushed in by a bullet," added Tom.

Just then a volley came from the besiegers, and a rain of bullets buried themselves in the trees behind which the boys were crouching.

Bart gave a sharp exclamation.

"Are you hurt, Bart?" asked Frank anxiously.

"Not much, I guess," replied Bart, putting his hand to his shoulder where the cloth had been torn away. "Just ridged the flesh. It doesn't amount to anything."

There was a little blood issuing from the shoulder, but Frank was relieved on examination to find that the bullet had just grazed the flesh, breaking the skin but doing no serious damage. He put a little ointment and lint on it and held the bandage firm with a bit of adhesive plaster, though Bart declared that it was not worth bothering about.

"Here they come!" cried Tom.

The besiegers had gathered themselves for a rush, and now they came in a body toward the trees, firing as they ran.

The rifles of the Army Boys spoke, and two of their assailants went down. The rest faltered for a moment, and in that moment another of their number fell.

This seemed to dash the spirit of the attackers. They had evidently counted upon the retreat of the defenders when they saw three times their number bearing down upon them. They faltered, then broke and ran, not this time to the nearest shelters, but straight back to the place from which they had first started. The accurate shooting had given them a wholesome respect for their opponents, and their only thought was to get out of the range of those deadly rifles.

The boys might have shot more of them as they ran, but that was not in Frank's plan. All he wanted was to get them out of his path so that he could get his prisoners to camp, and he wanted to do it with as little bloodshed as possible.

"Guess they've got enough of our game," remarked Tom, as he reloaded his rifle.

"Shouldn't wonder," replied Bart. "We called their bluff. They thought we'd have a case of nerves when we saw them come rushing towards us. But we've seen those fellows' backs too often to be afraid of their faces."

The Germans continued their retreat until they had gotten to a reasonably safe distance, and then they gathered together and seemed to be consulting as to their next move.

Frank watched them keenly. Suddenly he saw a commotion in their ranks, and looking in the direction to which their faces had turned, he saw a body of men larger than the first coming over the snow.

"Another bunch of disbanded soldiers," he muttered anxiously, as he saw that the newcomers were Germans and had now quickened their steps in answer to the shouts and gestures of their first assailants. "Now we're up against it for fair."

"We didn't figure on tackling the whole German army," growled Tom.

"Our ammunition is getting low, too," remarked Bart, ruefully, as he looked at his cartridge belt. "We'll have to make every shot tell from now on."

"If the bullets give out, we'll light into them with our bayonets and gun butts," gritted Frank between his teeth. "We've started to get these prisoners to camp, and we'll get them there or die trying."

"I know what the Germans would do if they were in our place," remarked Tom. "They'd stand the prisoners in front of them, so that the other fellows would have to kill their own comrades before they could get at them."

"I know they would," agreed Frank. "They did that in Belgium even with women and little children. But we're human beings, and we don't do that sort of thing."

By this time the two bodies of men had joined, and Frank estimated that altogether they numbered more than forty.

"Ten to one," he remarked when he had finished counting, "and most of those new arrivals have guns."

"We're in for another rush," said Bart, "and this time they won't cave in as easily as they did before. The Germans are plucky enough when they fight in numbers."

The Army Boys looked carefully to their rifles and loosened their knives in their sheaths. Then by a common impulse they shook hands all around. Nothing was said, but each knew what was in the hearts of the others. They felt that they were in for a fight to the death, and with the heavy odds against them it looked as though none of them would come out alive.

But the expected rush did not come.

"Can't be that they've given it up, do you think?" asked Tom, after five minutes had passed.

"Nothing like that," replied Frank. "They're holding a big pow-wow about something."

As he spoke, a figure detached itself from the crowd and came towards them, waving a white handkerchief attached to a stick.

"The white flag!" exclaimed Frank. "They're going to invite us to surrender."

"You know what Whittlesey told them in the Argonne when

they tried the same thing on the lost battalion," remarked Bart.

"We'll tell them the same thing, only a little more politely," Frank assured him with a grin.

The man approached until he was about fifty feet distant, and then stood there, waving the flag and by gestures inviting the defenders to come out and meet him.

"You're elected, Frank," laughed Billy. "Go out and let Heinie spiel his little spiel."

Frank laid aside his rifle and stepped from behind his tree. He walked directly toward the messenger, who lowered the makeshift flag and stood waiting.

"What is it that you want?" Frank asked in German, when he had come within speaking distance.

"We want you to surrender," replied the man in excellent English.

"And if we don't?" continued Frank, in his native tongue.

"Then you'll be committing suicide," answered the other promptly.

"I'm not so sure of that," replied Frank. "I suppose you'd have said that before you made your last rush. But as you see, we're not dead yet."

"That was different," replied the messenger. "You can see now that we have double the number we had before and more than double the guns. You can't possibly hold out against us."

"Maybe not," replied Frank, "but at any rate we're going to try. If you want us, you'll have to come and take us, and even then you'll only get our dead bodies, for we won't be taken alive."

He spoke with a decision that seemed to disconcert the man who stood for a moment irresolute.

"Is that your last word?" he asked.

"I have only one word," replied Frank. "You heard me. Go back and tell your comrades to come on as soon as they like. They'll find us ready for them. But I warn you now as I warned you before that our Government will get you—every last one of you. You may kill us, but you'll swing for it."

He turned to go back to his friends, but the messenger still stood there.

"Well," said Frank, turning around, "why don't you go? Got anything more to say?"

"Only this," returned the messenger. "My comrades will not insist on your surrender. But we must have the prisoners. If you give them up, you may go where you will."

"So you had that little joker in reserve, did you?" asked Frank grimly. "Well, my answer is just the same. We've got those prisoners, and we're going to keep them. We started to take them into camp, and we're going to take them there. If you get them at all, you'll get them after we're dead."

There was no mistaking the determination in his tones, and there was a look of unwilling admiration in the eyes of the messenger as he turned to depart.

"You are foolish," he said, "but you have had your chance. You and your companions are doomed."

"That may be," replied Frank, "but if we are, we'll take a lot of you along with us."

They separated and returned to their respective camps.

"Get ready now, boys, for the fight of your lives," Frank admonished his comrades, after he had told them of what had passed between him and the flag bearer.

"Let them come," said Bart. "We're good for a lot of them if our bullets hold out."

"And when they're gone, we've got our bayonets," put in Tom.

"And our knives may do some damage," added Billy, as his hand rested on the haft of his.

With every faculty alert and their eyes fixed upon their enemies, the Army Boys waited for the expected rush.

"What are they waiting for?" muttered Tom peevishly. "Are they getting cold feet? Or are they waiting for another gang of hoboes to join them before they care to tackle us?"

"It isn't that," Frank answered. "They may be planning new tactics. Their others didn't work very well."

"I believe they're going away," cried Billy, as he saw the crowd dispersing.

"Guess again," returned Frank. "They're doing what I've been afraid all along they'd try to do. They're spreading out so as to surround us on all sides. They didn't have men enough to do that at first, but they've got them now."

A few minutes more and they saw that Frank was right. The men were describing a wide circle, with the evident intention of attacking the Army Boys from all sides at once.

"That means that they'll drive us out into the open," said Frank. "We can't be on both sides of a tree at once. Half of them at least can take pot shots at us without our having any shelter."

"It's good dope from their point of view," remarked Tom. "We'd better start in to discourage it right away. They think they're out of range, but I'm going to try to prove to them that they're mistaken."

His eye ran along his rifle barrel, and after taking unusually careful aim he fired. One of the Germans threw up his hands and fell.

"A long shot, but I got him," remarked Tom with satisfaction.

"Some shot," said Bart approvingly.

The immediate result was a widening of the circle as the others tried to get back further out of range. But the circle kept forming just the same, and in a quarter of an hour it was completed.

Then it began contracting, the foe taking advantage of every hill and every tree to get nearer. Occasionally they would send over some scattering shots, but in the main they held their fire until they should get into closer quarters.

The Army Boys in the meantime had been working feverishly. The trees were no longer to be relied on, with enemies at the back as well as at the front. So they dug furiously into the snow, until they had heaped it high enough all around them to form a circular trench.

When they had finished, the top of the trench was on a level with their eyes, so that their bodies were sheltered. But they had to lift their heads above it as often as they sighted and fired their rifles, and they risked getting a bullet every time they did it.

By now the enemy was creeping closer, and there was a constant zipping of bullets around and over their heads. The boys themselves were forced to husband their fire, because of their scarcity of ammunition, and they wasted no bullets in merely returning the enemy's fire. They watched their opportunities, and wherever an arm or a head showed itself, it became a target for their rifles. Sometimes they missed, but oftener they found their mark, and they knew that they had put at least five of their enemies out of the fighting. But the odds were still enormous, and with every moment the Germans were drawing closer. Soon they would be near enough for a concerted rush from all sides at once.

"It's coming soon now, fellows," Frank warned his comrades, "and when it comes we want to jump out to meet it. We don't want to be caught in this trench like rats in a trap. When I give the word, let them have all you've got in your guns, and then we'll lay into them with our knives and bayonets."

Several minutes passed and the enemy's fire died down. Soon it ceased entirely and an ominous silence replaced the singing of the bullets.

"Have they run out of ammunition, do you think?" Bart

Homer Randall

asked of Frank.

"No such luck," was the answer. "They're getting ready for a rush. On your toes now, and listen for the word."

One, two, three minutes passed. And then came the rush.

But it was not the rush that the boys had looked for!

Out from the trees with a wild cheer came tearing a squad of the old Thirty-seventh, with Wilson at their head, and fell like an avalanche on the foe!

The Germans were taken completely by surprise. In their concentration on their expected prey they had failed to note the foe approaching from the rear. There were a few scattered shots, and then the Germans scattered and ran like so many hares in all directions.

CHAPTER IX

THE COLONEL'S WARNING

The Army Boys for the first instant were almost paralyzed with surprise. In their hearts they had bidden good-bye to the world, for they knew how slight their chances were against the odds that menaced them.

Frank was the first to grasp the situation, and he jumped from the trench with a wild hurrah.

"It's the old Thirty-seventh!" he yelled. "Our own boys! Come along, fellows!"

With a whoop Bart and Tom joined him, Billy remaining to guard his prisoners, and they plunged at once into the task of hunting down the fugitives. A few escaped through the wood, but the great majority of them were rounded up and placed in charge of Billy and several aids. Aid was given to the wounded, and litters were made for them which the prisoners were compelled to carry. There were two killed, and these were buried where they lay.

It was only after these necessary things had been attended to that the boys were able to get their breath and find time for explanations with Wilson, who was delighted beyond measure to find that apart from the trifling ridge in Bart's shoulder they were all safe and sound.

He listened with the utmost interest and attention while they unfolded the story of their adventures.

"It is a mighty fine piece of work you boys have done," he remarked, after he had fully grasped the situation, "They'll be glad at headquarters to have these conspirators under their thumb, for they've been hearing all sorts of queer things about ructions that are being planned in the occupied zone. So Raymond's stumble may prove to have been a good thing after all."

"Perhaps it was," admitted Bart with a grin, "though I've been calling myself all sorts of a boob ever since the thing happened."

"It sure has kept things from being monotonous," chuckled Billy. "I've had a lot of things happen to me in my young life, but I can't just now recall anything much more exciting than has taken place since we lost you last night in the snow."

"The lieutenant was all wrought up about it," said the corporal. "He had searching parties out for you all last night. Right after breakfast this morning he routed us out again and told us we'd hear from him if we came back without you."

"Well, you've got us, all right, and a nice little bunch of prisoners in addition to prove that we haven't been loafing on the job," laughed Frank. "But how did you come to find us?"

"It was the sound of shooting that brought us here on the double quick," replied Wilson. "We took just one look at that circle creeping up on you and we tumbled to the situation at once."

"You came just in the nick of time," said Bart soberly. "If you'd been five minutes later you wouldn't have found much except our dead bodies."

"And the old Thirty-seventh would have lost four of its best men," replied the corporal warmly. "But we'd better get a move on now and hustle back to camp."

He lined up his men, and after appointing guards for the disarmed and sullen prisoners, took up the march.

A little over an hour later the band trooped into the village where Lieutenant Winter's detachment was stationed. News of their coming had been carried on ahead, and they received a royal welcome from the men, who crowded about them and grasped their hands and pounded their backs as they made their way to headquarters.

There the reception was more than cordial, and there was heartfelt relief in the clean cut face of the lieutenant as he had the Army Boys tell their story.

"Fine work," he commented, when they had finished. "You men are a credit to the regiment and the army. I'll see that this is brought to the notice of the general in command. You can go now, that is, all but Sheldon. I'll need one of you here to check up on the stories of the prisoners."

The others saluted and retired, and while the prisoners were sent for the lieutenant looked over the map with great interest, asking Frank many questions about the speech he had heard in connection with it.

The man with the red beard simply admitted that his name

was Spatler, and then shut up like an oyster. No persuasion or threats could bring anything out of him, and he was finally sent back to the guardhouse to be eventually dealt with by the authorities at Coblenz. The mark of Billy's punch was still evident in his swollen jaw, and he shot a baleful glance at Frank as he passed by him on the way out.

Other prisoners were questioned without result, until the German was reached whom Frank had arrested at the point of his pistol. All his insolence and braggadocio had vanished. He was evidently a poltroon at heart, for he showed every evidence of being willing to betray his comrades and tell all that he knew on condition that his own lot would be made easier.

"This is getting interesting," smiled the lieutenant as he saw that the man was beginning to weaken. "I guess I'll excuse you now, Sheldon, for he'll probably talk more freely with me alone. And as he talks English I shan't need an interpreter."

Frank saluted and went out, glad to rejoin his comrades, whom he found regaling themselves with hot coffee and steaming "chow" which the company cook had put before them, a pleasure in which Frank himself promptly took part, while their comrades crowded around them eager to hear every detail of their experiences of the night before.

They had scarcely finished before Frank was summoned to headquarters by a messenger. He went, expecting that something had come up in connection with the prisoners, but was agreeably surprised to find his old friend, Colonel Pavet, waiting for him.

The meeting was especially cordial on both sides. Colonel Pavet had not forgotten how Frank had brought him in wounded from the battlefield under a hail of enemy fire, and Frank on his part had a profound gratitude to the colonel for his efforts to secure for Mrs. Sheldon her rights in her father's property.

"So you are still at it," smiled the colonel, after greetings had been exchanged.

"What do you mean?" asked Frank.

"Modest as usual," said the colonel. "I've been hearing all about the little war you've been carrying on on your own account. It was a gallant piece of work, and I congratulate you."

"Oh, that was nothing," replied Frank. "It was a job that came our way and we had to do it. But how comes it that I see you in this out of the way place?" he continued, in order to change the conversation.

"I have been to Berlin on a military commission for the Allies," replied the colonel, "and I am now on my way to Coblenz, from which city I will go to our own bridgehead at Mayence."

"So you got to Berlin, did you?" asked Frank with interest. "It's the place I've been wanting to get to ever since I've been in the war. But I wanted to go in with a conquering army with bugles blowing and drums beating and flags flying and plant the flags of the Allies on the Kaiser's palace."

"I have shared that ambition," replied the colonel, "and there's nothing in the world that could have kept us from doing it, if the Germans hadn't signed the armistice just when they did. But, for that matter, we may have to do it yet."

"Do you think so?" asked Frank with quickened interest.

"I shouldn't be surprised," was the reply. "Things are in a terrible condition there. The Soldiers' and Workmen's Councils are trying to take possession of the Government. There were street riots every day that I was there. The police station was captured by the rioters and scores of detectives and policemen were murdered by the mob. The buildings are riddled with bullets and cannon balls. Berlin is getting some of the punishment that is due for her guilt in starting the war."

"I suppose that fellow Liebknecht is at the head of all this," remarked Frank.

"He was, but he isn't any longer," replied Colonel Pavet.

"What do you mean?" asked Frank. "Has he been arrested?"

"He's been killed," was the answer.

"How did that happen?"

"He was shot while attempting to escape from the officers who were taking him to prison," said the colonel. "At least, that was the explanation given. More than likely that was only a pretext. But he is dead anyway, and so is that she-tigress, Rosa Luxemburg, who was his partner in stirring up the mobs. They sowed the wind of riot and massacre and now they have reaped the whirlwind."

"Well, now that they are killed I suppose things will quiet down somewhat," remarked Frank.

The colonel shook his head.

"I don't know," he said dubiously. "The mobs will probably try to obtain revenge for the killing of their leaders. Things look very black, not only in Berlin but in every part of the country. Business is paralyzed, millions are on strike, the food situation is bad, and the whole nation is mad with the bitterness of defeat."

"How about their signing the treaty?" asked Frank. "Do you think they will do it?"

"They say they won't," replied the colonel. "They are calling it all kinds of names, 'the graveside of right', 'the Peace of violence', 'the shackles of slaves' and all that kind of rot. They swear they will never sign it. But then you have to take that talk for what it is worth. The Germans are the greatest bluffers and the quickest quitters in the world. There is what you Americans call the 'yellow streak' all through the nation. They said they wouldn't sign the armistice, but they signed it. They said they'd never let us enter their territory, but we're here. Now they're saying they'll never sign the Peace Treaty, but they'll probably do it when it comes to the pinch. Outside they're tigers, but inside they're sheep."

"Well," said Frank, "I almost wish they wouldn't. I'd rather have the treaty signed at Berlin than at Versailles."

"Eager for more fighting with the Huns?" asked the colonel, with an amused smile.

"Not that exactly," returned Frank. "But when I start a job I like to finish it and finish it right."

"Well," said the colonel, "you may have all the fighting you want right here in the Coblenz bridgehead. I heard rumors when I was in Berlin that a movement was on foot to stir up trouble in the zone of American occupation. Agitators were to be sent there by the Spartacans to try to overthrow the local government and take the reins of power. I heard that proposed myself at a street meeting of rioters that I witnessed from the windows of my hotel. A man with a red beard was declaiming at the top of his lungs and predicting that if the people of Coblenz would rise under the red flag they could sweep the hated Americans back from the Rhine."

"A man with a red beard, did you say?" asked Frank.

"Why, yes," answered the colonel, a little amused by his earnestness. "Not that there's anything extraordinary about that, I should suppose. There are probably thousands of men with red beards in Berlin. Why do you ask?"

"Because," said Frank, "the man whom we captured in the ruined castle last night and whom the lieutenant has been examining also has a red beard. He is an agitator of the worst type, and I know from what he said in his speech that he comes from Berlin. It may be only a coincidence, but if so it's a singular one."

"I shouldn't wonder if you were right," said the colonel. "What is the man's name?"

"Spatler, I think," replied Frank. "Heinrich Spatler. At any rate that's the name he gave to the lieutenant."

"Spatler," repeated the colonel, wrinkling his brows. "It seems to me that I saw that name on one of the banners carried by the rioters at the meeting. It may be that you are right. If he's the same man, he's a fanatic of the most dangerous kind and will stop at nothing. I hope that now your people have him under lock and key you'll keep him there. But I must go now, as I want to reach Mayence to-night if possible. I'm very glad to have had this few minutes' chat with you. By the way, when have you heard from Madame Sheldon? I hope that she is well."

"I had a letter from her a week ago," replied Frank. "She is in excellent health and full of gratitude to you for your efforts in recovering her property. As soon as I am released from the Army of Occupation she plans to meet me in Paris and go with me to Auvergne. There she will have a chance to meet you and express her thanks in person."

"I shall be charmed," replied the colonel. "I should like nothing better than to have her settle in France permanently as a resident of our beautiful Auvergne, but I suppose that is too much to hope for. You have America in your blood."

"Yes," laughed Frank. "France is beautiful and great, but America is to me above all."

"I should think less of you if it were not so," answered Colonel Pavet. "*Au revoir,* then. Remember me to Madame Sheldon when you write."

With a cordial handshake they parted. The colonel vaulted into the saddle of his horse which an orderly was holding at the door, and Frank returned to his comrades, who he found busily preparing to return to Coblenz, in accordance with an order that had just come from the lieutenant.

"Why we've just got here!" objected Frank, when he heard the news. "And now we're going back!"

"It's this way," explained Tom. "The lieutenant is anxious to get those prisoners off his hands and safe in jail at Coblenz. It seems that he pumped a lot of information out of one of the fellows who gave away his comrades, and he wants headquarters to go into the matter at once. We've been chosen among others to guard the prisoners because we took them and we may be wanted as witnesses. So back we go, and I'm glad of it."

"Same here," echoed Billy.

Bart and Frank looked at each other and laughed.

"'Alice, where art thou?'" quoted Bart.

"We know why you fellows want to get back to Coblenz in such a hurry," joked Frank. "Gee, it must be awful to have such a hankering. I will admit, however, that Alice and Helen are pretty girls. Bless you, my children, bless you."

"Quit your kidding and get busy," admonished Billy. "We start in half an hour."

"We'll be ready," replied Frank. "Watch our smoke."

At the appointed hour all was ready and the company set off with their prisoners under guard. There was a strong detachment as escort, and in addition to the men's rifles, a couple of machine guns were taken along, as the lieutenant was taking no chances. He had learned enough from the perusal of the papers and the testimony of the informer to believe that serious trouble was brewing, and he was anxious above all that the prisoners should be safely delivered at Coblenz.

It was a beautiful winter day. The air, though cold, was still, and the sun was shining brightly. The boys were in high spirits and joked and laughed as they trudged along. The prisoners alone were sullen and depressed. The man with the red beard was the only one that maintained an air of defiant.

Suddenly, the roar of an aeroplane made itself heard, and, looking up, the boys descried it sailing above them like a gigantic bird and moving in the same direction in which they were traveling. They saw at a glance that it was an American plane.

"No more need to duck for shelter when we see those things," laughed Billy.

"No bombs coming down to smash us into bits," exulted Bart.

"No," said Frank, "all German planes are on the ground. They can't look for Red Cross signs and hospitals any more."

"This fellow's swooping down!" exclaimed Tom, with heightened interest. "Maybe he's caught sight of us fellows and wants to get a closer look."

CHAPTER X

FROM THE SKY

"More likely it's engine trouble of some kind," suggested Frank, gazing at the swooping airplane. "My, but he's a nifty driver! See how he handles that machine!"

"Dick Lever himself couldn't do better," remarked Bart, as he watched the graceful curves described by the aviator in his descent.

"Good old Dick!" observed Billy. "I wonder where he is now."

The aviator was evidently aiming for a large open space a little to the right and in advance of the moving column. Soon he had reached it and landed as lightly as a feather.

"Wouldn't have broken a pane of glass if it had come down on it," observed Tom admiringly. "That fellow knows his business."

The aviator climbed out of his machine and came over toward the column, which had just received the order for the ten minutes rest, which, according to regulations, came at the end of every hour of marching.

He was encased in heavy clothing and his face was almost concealed by the fur-rimmed visor that he wore.

"Something about that fellow that looks familiar," remarked Billy.

"By the great horn spoon!" ejaculated Frank, "it's Dick Lever himself."

"That's what," smiled the newcomer, as the boys surrounded him and, with a yell, fell upon him.

There was no mistaking the warmth of the greeting, and Dick smiled with gratification as he extricated himself from their grasp and tried to shake hands with them all at once.

"What good wind blew you this way?" queried Frank.

"A mighty cold wind, as you fellows would admit if you were up there," laughed Dick.

"You look pretty well fixed for it," commented Billy, as he took in Dick's voluminous trappings. "A polar bear has nothing on you."

"I need every bit of it," answered Dick. "But where are you fellows bound for, and what are you doing with these birds?" he continued, glancing at the motley group of prisoners.

"We're taking them into Coblenz to let our people give them the once over and the third degree," explained Frank. "They've been trying to stir up trouble in the American zone. Cunning little bunch, isn't it?"

"I'm glad you've got your claws on them," Dick remarked, looking at the group with cold disfavor. "There's a whole lot more like them that ought to be rounded up. I tell you our people have been too easy with this breed of cattle and they're going to be sorry for it. We're so afraid of being harsh that we go to the other extreme. We stand up so straight that we fall over backward. The Germans don't understand anything but force, and unless we exert it they think we're afraid to."

"Think we're too easy?" asked Bart. "You bet we are!" replied Dick. "We ought to treat them as the French do at Mayence and the British at Cologne. They know the people they're dealing with, and while they're just, they're stern. Anyone who tries to put anything over on them finds that he's monkeying with a buzz saw. Unless we wake up from our easy good-nature, we'll find ourselves with a lot of trouble on our hands."

"You seem to be rather worked up about it," remarked Billy.

"Not a bit more than I ought to be," returned Dick earnestly. "I have chances of seeing things that you fellows don't. I'm flying all over the occupied zone, and I tell you that the Spartacides are trying to stir up trouble everywhere. In almost every other town you can see the red flag flying. There's stormy weather coming, and we've got to be prepared for gales."

"That just fits in with what Colonel Pavet of the French Army was telling me to-day," said Frank. "He's just back from Berlin, and he's sure there's trouble afoot."

"Well," said Dick, "I hope that we're both false prophets, but I'm afraid we're not. I'll have to get on now, fellows."

"What did you come down for?" asked Tom. "Engine trouble?"

"No, it wasn't that," replied Dick. "The old girl is working fine. I just saw an American bunch marching along here and dropped down to say 'howdy.' I'm off now. See you soon in Coblenz."

With a wave of his hand, he walked over, climbed into his machine, and started skyward.

The boys watched him soaring until his machine was only a dot in the steel blue of the winter sky, and then, as their brief rest period had ended, started on the march to Coblenz.

"One great boy, that Dick," remarked Frank, when the aviator was finally lost to sight.

"You bet he is," agreed Billy emphatically. "He's one of the greatest aces that ever climbed into a plane."

"I suppose he must be feeling rather lonely now that he isn't bringing down his daily Hun," suggested Tom.

"He's all wool and a yard wide," affirmed Bart. "I'll never forget that if it hadn't been for him I might never have got back to you fellows."

"Do you remember the time he swooped down with his machine guns popping and carried us off when we were being taken to a German prison camp?" asked Frank. "I tell you it took nerve for a fellow to charge a whole detachment."

"Oh, he's got nerve enough for a whole regiment," declared Billy. "He'd be a mighty handy fellow to have at your back in any kind of scrap, and don't you forget it."

In a short time they reached the town without further adventure and delivered their prisoners into the hands of the authorities. They were off duty then and had no further assignment for the rest of the afternoon and evening. The early winter dusk was settling down, but it was yet a full hour before it would be entirely dark.

"What are you going to do with yourself, Bart?" asked Frank. "I know of course what Tom and Billy are going to do. They're going to make tracks for the house where their deities reside."

"Good guess," admitted Billy. "You bet we are."

"I haven't anything special on hand," replied Bart in answer to Frank's question.

"Come along with me then," said his chum.

"Anywhere you say, what's the game?"

"I'm going straight for the alley where they nearly got our number the other night. That thing's on my mind all the time. It haunts me even in my sleep. I'm going to get to the bottom of that mystery or know the reason why."

"All right. I'm with you."

By the time they had reached the alley it was almost entirely dark. Choosing a moment when the street was empty, they slipped into the alley and made their way toward the further end.

They felt the walls on either side as they went along for indications of a door or opening of any kind. They did the same with the blank wall that closed the alley at the other end. Nothing rewarded their search. The wall at the farther end was far too high to scale. It seemed impossible for anything except with wings to vanish from the alley as completely as had their assailants on that memorable night when they had so nearly lost their lives.

"It beats me," said Bart at length. "We saw them go in and we followed them up and they weren't there. Sounds like black magic, doesn't it?"

"It surely does," agreed Frank, in great perplexity. "They didn't go through the back, they couldn't go through the sides, they couldn't go into the air, but they did go somewhere."

"Down into the ground," suggested Bart jokingly. "That seems the only place left."

Frank started.

"There's many a true word spoken in jest," he said. "Perhaps you've hit it, Bart. That's one place we haven't examined."

"Small chance to examine that just now," said Bart. "You can see it's all covered with a glare of ice. There isn't a bit of ground showing."

They walked over the ice-covered surface with scarcely a hope under present conditions of making any discoveries, even if there were any to make. They had to depend entirely upon the sense of touch, for it was by this time pitch dark and Frank did not care to flash his light for fear they might be observed by passers-by.

They had come perhaps to within twenty feet of the rear wall, when Frank gave a sudden exclamation.

CHAPTER XI

MARSHAL FOCH AND GENERAL PERSHING

"What is it, Frank?" asked Bart Raymond in a low voice.

"My foot sank in," explained Frank. "It's softer here for some reason than in the rest of the alley. Just wait a minute till I can feel around here and see what I can make of it."

He felt about cautiously with his feet and found that the ice had softened for a space of about four feet and that the space was almost perfectly square.

"There's some reason why this spot should be different from the rest," he said, after having verified his discovery. "It's all open to the weather, like every other part of the alley, and there's only one explanation. There's heat coming up from beneath. That means that there must be an open space beneath this spot. I wish I dared use my flashlight."

"Wait a minute," said Bart. "I'll slip out to the mouth of the alley and see if the coast is clear. If it is, I'll give a low whistle and then you flash your light and see what it shows you."

He left his companion, and a moment after Frank heard the

signal agreed upon.

Instantly he flashed his light on the rectangular space that had caught his attention.

The ice had melted there to such an extent that only a thin glaze covered the surface. Through this transparent covering Frank Sheldon caught sight of what seemed to be the outline of a door covered with gravel that only partially concealed it. He thought he saw something too that faintly resembled an iron ring.

"A trap door!" he muttered under his breath, jubilant in the thought that he had perhaps fallen upon a clue to the mystery that had so long perplexed him.

He took out his knife and began to dig down toward the ring, when a low whistle from the opening to the alley warned him to be on the alert. Instantly the light was extinguished and the next moment Bart was at his side.

"Better let up, Frank," he whispered. "There's a big commotion down the street and a crowd is beginning to gather. I think it's a fire."

As he spoke, a fire engine clanged down the street and an increasingly red light made itself apparent in the sky.

"Too bad," grumbled Frank, as he put his flashlight back into his pocket "I think I was just on the verge of finding out something that would put us on the track of those fellows who seemed to vanish into thin air."

"Hard luck," murmured Bart, sympathetically, "but well have to give it up for the present."

Frank hesitated, but the increasing glare that made the alley visible and the sound of footsteps of people hurrying to the fire showed him that his friend was right, and he reluctantly desisted.

"To-morrow's a new day," said Bart consolingly, as the comrades stole out of the alley and mingled with the groups of passers-by.

"If Tom and Billy can tear themselves away from the girls, we'll bring them with us the first chance we get and try to clear up the whole mystery," observed Frank.

But this proved more difficult than they expected, and many days were to pass before their discovery could be followed up. There was a sudden tightening of the military regulations, which the boys attributed in part at least to the revelations that had followed the examination of their prisoners. A rigorous system of drill and training was put in force and the Army Boys' hours of liberty were greatly curtailed in consequence. They were kept more closely to their barracks, and their visits to the town except in the line of duty became few and far between.

The day following Frank's discovery that company of the old Thirty-seventh to which the boys belonged was sent on a long hike in full marching equipment, and when they returned after several hours they were, as Tom expressed it, "dog-tired." Nor were they pleased to find that in the interval their quarters had been changed and they had been assigned to another part of the barracks.

It was with sighs of relief that they eased their heavy packs from their shoulders and dropped them thumping to the floor.

"Gosh!" exclaimed Billy, "I don't mind carrying a pack that weighs sixty pounds or even eighty; but after a time this pack of mine gets to weigh about two tons, and that seems just a little bit too much."

"You told a whole bookful that time," said Tom ruefully. "It is surprising how those packs keep getting heavier all the time. Another half mile, and I think the straps would have been through my shoulders altogether."

"Well, there's no use worrying about what might have happened," laughed Frank, "seeing that we've arrived safe and sound. While we're in barracks we'll be able to get three square meals a day, and that appeals to me more, even, than getting rid of the old pack."

Frank had hardly finished speaking when an officer approached and called: "Attention!" Then followed roll call, and the boys, together with a number of their comrades, were assigned to a barracks next but one to that in which they had stopped. This, of course, necessitated shouldering the heavy packs once more, but by this time the boys had come to expect things like this, so took it all as a matter of course, and soon found themselves in the quarters that were to be theirs until the order came once more to march.

The barracks was furnished with rows of army cots, and the boys dropped their packs at the heads of those assigned to them. Then began the task of unpacking, and by the time that was completed it was almost time for mess.

"It's lucky we got our mess kits out before mess call blew," commented Tom. "It would be an awful thing to get caught without them around meal time."

"Not much danger of that," said Billy, with a mischievous

twinkle in his eye. "We've been in the army quite some time now, Tom, and yet I can't call to mind a single time when you weren't Johnny on the spot when the bugle blew for eats."

"Say, don't you two fellows go to starting an argument along those lines," interrupted Bart. "When it comes to being chow hounds, I think we're all tarred with the same brush. None of us has ever got a call from the mess sergeant for not being on time."

"Well, perhaps you're right," admitted Tom laughingly. "And when you get right down to it, the whole of this man's army seems to be about the same way, so that leaves nothing for us to argue about."

Mess kits in hand, they all trooped down to the kitchen and took their places on the line that already was of sizable length. They wound slowly past the cooks, and in course of time the four friends were served and fell to on a savory plate of substantial food.

For a short time conversation ceased, the boys giving their whole- hearted attention to the entertainment that Uncle Sam had provided. The food disappeared with astonishing rapidity, and when the last of it was gone Billy exclaimed:

"Fellows, we can kick all we want to over army life, but I never had such an appetite in civilian life, and never felt half as good as I do right this minute."

"All right, then, since you like it," grinned Frank, "to-morrow I'll let you carry my pack as well as your own, and then you'll feel just twice as good as you do now."

"No, thanks," declined Billy. "I don't want to feel any better than I do now. If I felt any better, I'd go to the medical officer to find out what was wrong with me."

"If you ate much more, you'd have a quartermaster officer coming around to find out what was the matter with you," countered Tom.

"The trouble with you is, that you don't understand my motives," complained Billy. "Personally, I dislike food, and, if I had my way, would make a canary bird look like a heavy eater. But I feel that it's my duty to eat a lot so that I can keep up my strength and continue to be a terror to all Germans. Uncle Sam expects this of me, and I refuse to disappoint him."

"Oh, well, if that's your motive, it's all right," said Tom, with mock gravity. "But seeing you in action, it looked to me as though you really enjoyed your grub. I hope you'll excuse my mistake."

"Oh, that's all right, please don't mention it," said Billy, with a magnanimous wave of his hand. "I've known others to make the same mistake, but, believe me or not, they don't always accept my statements as you do, when I explain the true state of affairs to them."

"Some people are hard to convince, I suppose," replied Tom, "but I guess I'm one of the easy ones."

"It's easier for both of you to talk than to wash mess gear apparently," said Frank, "What do you say to canning some of that brilliant repartee so that we can get these things out of the way and have time for a little something else before taps blow?"

"Suits me," acquiesced Billy. "But it surely does make me

feel bad to have people think I really like to eat, and I can't seem to rest easy until I set them right. But now, let's get these things cleaned up in a little less than no time."

It did not take long for the boys to get their mess kits cleaned and out of the way, and then they found themselves with a couple of hours to spend exactly as they pleased.

"Might as well wander over toward the canteen and see what's doing," suggested Frank, and as none of the others had anything better to propose, they acted accordingly.

At the canteen all was life, bustle and activity, one line always going in to purchase tobacco, candy, and such other little comforts as were on sale, and another coming out in possession of these valued commodities. It was hard to realize that all these men were tried and seasoned fighters, ready to "go and get the Hun at the drop of a hat."

"What's doing in the way of a camp entertainment to-night?" asked Frank of one burly doughboy, who was contentedly munching a huge piece of cake.

"I understand there's going to be a movie show," replied the latter. "They generally have pretty good reels too, so I'd advise you not to miss it."

"Much obliged," said Frank. "Guess we might as well take it in, fellows, what do you say?" turning to his companions.

"Sure thing," they assented, and accordingly made their way to a brightly lighted tent, toward which many others were going. They arrived there only a short time before the show was to start, and having secured good seats, settled down to enjoy it.

The scene of the picture was in the West, when it was still "wild and woolly," and depicted many encounters between settlers and Indians. These fights were the subject of much criticism by the expert audience, who did not hesitate to shout words of advice at critical situations.

"Gosh!" growled one doughboy, in deep disgust, "just one machine gun would have cleaned up that bunch of redskins in less time than it takes a Hun to say *'kamerad'*"

"Yes, or a few good hand grenades would have done their business for them, too," said another. "It's too bad the old timers didn't have a few of those modern playthings along. It would have made things a whole lot easier for them."

"What would have been the matter with a few tankfuls of poison gas?" suggested Bart. "Seems to me that would have made them curl up and quit pretty quick."

There were other suggestions of the same nature, and when the picture finally came to a close there was a general impression that such warfare was mild indeed compared to that of the present day.

"I don't know how you fellows feel," remarked Frank, as they filed out of the tent and started for their barracks, "but I feel tired enough to crawl into my little two by four and get a real night's sleep."

"I'm with you," declared Tom. "I felt all right before, but that picture seems to have made me tired, because now it's all I can do to stay awake."

"I guess it must have been the picture all right," said Billy, "because certainly it isn't because of overwork."

"Well, I didn't claim it was from overwork, did I?" replied Tom. "I enlisted in the Army to fight Germans, not to work. All I've had to do is march twenty or thirty miles a day with a sixty pound pack on my back, but outside of that I must admit that I didn't do much work, except dig trenches, do sentry duty, and kill a few Huns as a sideline. It certainly is one grand picnic for me, I don't mind admitting."

"Yes, and to make you like it all the more," said Billy, "I hear that there's going to be big doings to-morrow—a review, plenty of marching and maneuvering to give the soldiers a good time, and it is expected a pleasant day will be had by all."

"You might know something like that would happen just when we think we're laid up for a nice rest," grumbled Tom. "But maybe it will rain, and then the whole thing will have to be called off."

But Tom's hope was a vain one, for the next day broke clear and delightful, with never a suggestion of rain in the heavens. Reveille blew at its accustomed unearthly time, according to the soldiers' standpoint, and the boys could soon tell that something was "in the wind" by the air of suppressed excitement on every hand.

"Guess you were right, Billy," said Tom, who had not as yet fully recovered from his grouch of the previous evening. "I thought when the armistice was signed that we would be all through with this sort of thing, but I suppose I should have known better."

"We're not through with it yet, and what's more, we won't be through with it for some time to come," said Frank. "Remember, the peace treaty isn't signed yet, and in Berlin they say they're not going to sign it. And it's just a case of where we can't let up until they do."

"As far as I'm concerned, I wish they wouldn't sign it," said Bart. "We stopped fighting too soon, anyway. We should have kept on until we'd carried the war on to German territory. It would do me good to see their cities get a dose of the same medicine they handed out to French and Belgian towns."

"There's a lot of people feel the same way," agreed Frank. "But before we get through with them I think they'll realize that they've got the loser's end of the proposition."

Just as Frank ceased speaking the bugle blew general assembly, and the boys hastened to fall into ranks. The officers paced up and down the lines, straightening them out and inspecting clothing and equipment as they went along. Then their captain appeared on the scene and proceeded to make them a short address.

"Men," he said, "the regiment is going to be inspected by General Pershing to-day, and I hardly need to tell every one of you to be right up on his toes. I know you can pass a perfect inspection, and it's up to every man to be a credit to the regiment."

After the captain had left the officer next in charge supplemented his word.

"You are going to be dismissed now, and will have a chance to get thoroughly cleaned up and ready for inspection," he said. "Any man that isn't in first class shape by the time assembly blows again is going to find himself out of luck. Dismissed!"

Everybody saluted, and the Army Boys joined in the rush

back to the barracks. The next hour was a busy one, in which razors, combs and brushes were applied vigorously, and the man with a complete shoe cleaning outfit found himself suddenly popular. The scene in the crowded washrooms resembled pandemonium let loose, but in an incredibly short time first one man and then another emerged spic and span, and by the time the bugle blew again there were only a few stragglers who were caught unprepared. These last threw themselves desperately into their uniforms, and two minutes after the bugle sounded every man was standing in his appointed place.

Then followed the preliminary inspection, after which the command "at ease" was given. Everybody shifted to a more comfortable position, and prepared for the long delay that they knew would probably ensue.

"Wonder how long it will be before the general arrives," speculated Frank. "It's only about half past nine now, and I don't believe he'll get here anything like that early."

"He'll probably have lunch first," predicted Tom, gloomily. "They've just got us out here now with the idea that standing will make us grow."

"Aw, snap out of it," laughed Billy. "I knew a man once that died from an in growing grouch, and likely enough the same thing will happen to you."

"It's just like an in growing toenail, only worse," chuckled Bart.

"Can't help it," said Tom. "This sort of thing is enough to give any one a grouch. Chances are that General Pershing has forgotten all about us, and we'll have to stand here until we starve to death."

"Well, you haven't got to worry about that just yet," said Bart, "because you haven't much more than gotten through your breakfast. Why—"

But he was interrupted by the short blast on the bugle that signified "attention," and everybody straightened like a flash. A big gray automobile pulled up in front of headquarters, and from it descended the general, accompanied by officers of his staff. Punctilious salutes were exchanged, and then the general, accompanied by some of his officers and also those of the regiment, passed slowly between the long files of straight-backed soldiers. His searching glance seemed to take in everything at once, but so thoroughly had every one prepared that even his exacting eye could find nothing to take exception to. It was a time of suspense for all the soldiers, as they knew that the least detail of dress or equipment lacking or misplaced meant a visit to the guardhouse. But the inspection passed off perfectly, as far as the men were concerned, and soon the inspecting party turned its attention to the barracks. The men were still held in ranks at attention, however, as nobody knew what the next step in the day's events would be.

Not long after the inspecting party had disappeared into the barracks they reappeared and made their way to regimental headquarters. Here they formed in a group, and, as far as the boys could judge, appeared to be awaiting the arrival of some person or persons, as they kept glancing down the road over which the general's car had come only a short time before.

"They must be expecting some other big bugs," speculated Billy in a whisper, keeping at the same time a wary eye on the nearest officer. "Looks as though this were going to be a red letter day around these diggings."

Homer Randall

Sure enough, Billy had hardly enunciated the words when another big military car appeared, dashing up to headquarters at high speed and stopping with a jerk. Great was the curiosity as to whom the last comer might be, and greater still the surprise when the soldiers recognized the well known features of the commander-in- chief of all the Allied armies, Marshal Foch himself!

To the boys the reason for the great marshal's presence here was obscure, but, as usual, his movements were dictated by very sufficient reasons. He was preparing the future movements of the Allied armies in the event of Germany's refusal to sign the peace treaty. Where a civilian might have said: "Oh, of course they'll sign the treaty; what else can they do?" the man who had led the Allies to victory had no intention of leaving the smallest thing to chance. At present he was making an inspection of all the Allied armies at the Rhine crossings, together with their equipment, transportation facilities, artillery, and all the other branches on which a successful advance would so much depend.

After a short conversation in the open, Marshal Foch and General Pershing entered the regimental headquarters, accompanied by the higher officers of both staffs. Meanwhile the boys had again been given the command "at rest," which was a welcome change from the long period of standing rigidly at attention.

After a short interval, the two generalissimos reappeared. This time both entered the car that had brought Marshal Foch to the scene, and the big automobile rolled off in a cloud of dust.

"Guess inspection is over now, and pretty near time, too," whispered Tom.

His surmise turned out to be correct, for shortly afterward the regiment was dismissed and returned to the barracks, where shortly afterward the midday mess was served.

But the visit of the two commanders marked the beginning of an era of extreme bustle and activity. Numbers of tanks, both small and large, began to make their appearance in the camp, likewise heavily loaded ammunition wagons and lorries, big field pieces, and all the other equipment that modern warfare has made a necessity.

Of course all this was of the greatest interest to the four Army Boys, as to their comrades, and many were the speculations as to its meaning.

"Looks as though the war had started again," said Bart. "There hasn't been as much as this stirring since the armistice was signed."

"Either that, or we're getting all ready to start again, which seems more likely to me. But we'll probably find out soon enough, one way or another," remarked Billy.

It was in fact the preparation of a new drive that they saw going on about them. And this time, should it start, the drive would not stop its easterly course until it reached Berlin. The Allied leaders were determined to make this advance so irresistible and conclusive that there could be no discussion afterward as to whether the German Army really was beaten.

More men and supplies arrived constantly. Two days after the visit of Marshal Foch and General Pershing a number of aeroplanes arrived, and a flying field was established adjoining the main camp. Here a number of observation balloons were continually being tried out, and it was seldom that one was not hovering over the camp.

"That's one thing," fellows, that we have yet to try," said Frank, addressing his friends. "We've been in the tanks, up in aeroplanes, and about every other place you can think of except a 'sausage' balloon. It would suit me fine to go up in one and get a bird's-eye view of 'the Rhine, the Rhine, the German Rhine.'

CHAPTER XII

TORN FROM MOORINGS

"No accounting for tastes," grinned Billy Waldon, "but as for me I'd rather have a sausage in me than to be in a sausage."

Little more was said about going up in the observation balloons at that time, but the same evening after colors, as the four friends all happened to be off duty at the same time, they decided to stroll over to the aviation field, as that seemed to offer more things of interest than any other place. As they drew near, they saw that one of the balloons was just being inflated, and they quickened their steps. A few hundred paces brought them alongside the partly inflated balloon, which already was tugging strongly at its moorings as the buoyant gas hissed into it. The observer who was to go up in it was standing near, and seeing the interest the boys took in the process, he bestowed a friendly grin on them.

"Thinking of going into the business?" he inquired gaily.

"Don't know but what I might some day," replied Frank, in the same vein. "What are the inducements?"

"Well, if you happen to have any troubles on your mind, this is pretty apt to end them all for you, once and for all. I can't give you any testimonials from others who have used this cure, because after they took it they weren't giving testimonials any more, but I give you my word that it's all that I claim for it"

"Yes, but you've been up quite a few times probably, and you're still in the land of the living so it can't be quite as bad as you say it is," replied Frank, laughingly.

"Oh, it's safe enough now, as far as that goes," said the other. "But when actual fighting is going on, then it's a different matter altogether."

"Were you ever attacked while you were up?" asked Billy.

"I surely was," replied the observer. "I was up over No Man's Land one day, right on the edge of the clouds, when suddenly a Boche airplane came darting out of the clouds and opened on me with his machine gun before I knew what had happened. Just by luck, I didn't get hit, but the bullets tore big holes in the balloon and it started to drop fast. I had time to jump clear with my parachute though, and landed without a scratch not a hundred feet from the wreckage of my balloon."

"You were pretty lucky, at that," observed Billy.

"You bet I was!" assented the other. "Another time I had to jump for it, too; only this time the balloon caught fire from some incendiary bullets fired at it. After I jumped the parachute was mighty slow in acting, and I dropped two thirds of the way before it finally took hold. I gave myself up for lost that time, and, as it was, I landed so hard that my left leg was broken, but even at that I wasn't doing much kicking."

"No, you wouldn't, with a leg broken," observed Billy slyly.

"That's one on me," conceded the observer, with a laugh. "At the time, though, I couldn't see much humor in it. Take it altogether, I guess a balloon will give a man his fair share of thrills."

"Gosh! I'd like to try it once," said Frank, longingly.

"If you'd really like to try it so much, I don't know but what I can arrange it for you," said the observer slowly. "The trouble is, though, that I can take only two of you, because I have only two extra parachutes."

"We're not apt to need them, are we?" asked Frank.

"Oh, of course, the chances are that we won't, seeing that we won't be attacked now by a hostile machine, as we would likely have been a few months ago," responded the other. "Just the same, it's always possible for accidents to happen, and so I'll have to limit it to two passengers, although I'd like to take you all up."

"You and Bart go, Frank," said Billy. "Tom and I will come around some other time, and then maybe we'll get a chance."

"Well, if you and Tom don't mind, I guess we will," said Frank, and with the words he and Bart stepped into the car of the balloon, followed by the observer.

"I'm afraid you'll find it rather tame," said the latter. "It's not nearly as exciting as you might think when looking at it from the ground."

By this time the balloon was fully inflated, and the observer gave the sign to the man in charge of the windlass to let the big gas bag rise. The windlass man released the brake on the big drum, and the balloon shot upward with a speed that took the breath away from the two passengers. Up they shot until they had attained an altitude of about five hundred feet, after which the windlass man checked their further progress.

The boys exclaimed aloud over the wonderful sight that met their eyes. Mile upon mile the smiling Rhine countryside stretched away on every side. The picturesque Rhine, bordered by its ruined castles, was visible for many miles.

"Isn't that a wonderful sight?" demanded Bart. "Why, from up here it seems as though we should almost be able to see Berlin."

"From the way things look now," observed their newly found friend grimly, "we'll all see Berlin pretty soon, and we won't have to go up in balloons to see it, either."

"Right you are!" acquiesced Bart. "And I'd be one happy little soldier if I knew that we were going to start to-morrow."

While the foregoing dialogue had been going on Frank had been taking in the view, but now he turned to the observer.

"Seems to me it looks pretty black over in the west," he remarked. "I think we're going to have a storm."

The observer glanced quickly in the direction indicated, and then jumped for his telephone.

"Pull her down, Dan!" he called. "Pull her down quick! There's a big storm coming our way, and coming mighty fast, too."

The boys could feel the tug of the cable as it tightened in response to the starting of the windlass, but before the balloon had descended a hundred feet the storm was upon them. A mighty blast roared about the frail balloon, jerking it here and there in such a violent manner that the boys were nearly thrown out. The captive balloon tore madly at its moorings, and seemed like some wild thing struggling to be free.

"We're in for it now," yelled Dunton, the observer. "She won't stand much more of this, and if she breaks away, it's the parachutes for us."

Even as he spoke a specially vicious blast tore madly at the balloon, and the occupants heard a ripping, tearing sound. A second later the big "sausage" leaped upward, and the boys did not need to be told that it had broken free from its moorings.

"Get hold of the parachutes!" yelled Dunton, "but don't jump yet. This wind is too strong, but if it dies down a little we'll have to risk it."

They were traveling at a terrific rate before the wind, and mounting steadily higher. Instead of abating, the wind seemed momentarily to increase in violence, and the balloon made increasingly heavier weather of it. It was only a matter of time when the wind would rip it to pieces, and this catastrophe was not long in coming. There was a sound of ripping cloth, and the next moment the balloon began to drop rapidly. This left its passengers no alternative but to take to their parachutes, as to remain longer with the balloon spelled sure death, and they had a bare chance for life if they jumped.

Grasping the hand-holds of the big white parachutes, the

three youths climbed to the edge of the basket, poised for a second, and then leaped off into space.

For seconds the Army Boys experienced a terrible series of sensations as they dropped with the speed of light toward the uprushing earth. The wind roared and whistled in their ears, and they both thought the parachutes would never open in time to prevent their being dashed to atoms on the ground. But when they were less than two hundred feet from the ground, each felt a sudden checking of the plummet-like drop and knew that the parachutes had at last taken hold. Slower and more slowly they went, as the parachutes gathered the air in their silken folds. But still the boys were not safe, for the strong wind tore at the parachutes and threatened at any moment to tear them loose. But at last Frank landed, with considerable of a shock, to be sure, but free of serious injury. His first thought was of his companions, and especially of Bart.

By great good fortune, Frank had landed clear of a river, although within a hundred feet of the bank. Looking in that direction, he was horrified to see Bart in the water, struggling amid the envelope and ropes of the parachute. He was so badly entangled that it was almost impossible for him to swim, and already his efforts were growing weaker.

Leaping to his feet, Frank rushed toward the stream, calling words of encouragement to his friend as he went.

"Hold up, Bart!" he yelled, "I'll be with you in a minute."

Reaching the river bank, he paused only long enough to kick off his shoes, and then plunged in to the rescue of his friend. With powerful strokes he plowed through the water, and was soon alongside Bart, who by this time was in sore straits.

Frank drew his knife, and with a few swift strokes cut away the wreckage of the parachute in which Bart was entangled.

"Thanks, old man," gasped the latter. "You came just in the nick of time, this time. Two minutes more, and I'd have been done for."

"Thank Heaven I did get here in time," said Frank fervently. "Just rest your hand on my shoulder, Bart, and I'll tow you to shore. It's lucky this river isn't as wide as the old Hudson, isn't it?"

Fortunately Frank was a powerful swimmer, and it did not take him long to reach the bank. He and Bart crawled up to dry land, and threw themselves panting on the ground to recover from their late misadventures. But a moment later, Frank was on his feet once more.

"I forgot all about Dunton, the observer!" he exclaimed. "He may have landed in the river, too, or he may be injured and in need of help. Do you feel fit enough to help me look for him, Bart?"

"Oh, I'm as good as ever now," said Bart, with an attempt at a grin. "Guess I must have been born to be hung, because I don't seem to be able to get myself killed by any other method."

The boys set out on their quest, and were soon delighted to see the observer himself limping toward them. The latter caught sight of them at the same time, and waved his hand to them.

"Gosh, but I'm glad to see you!" he exclaimed, when they came within speaking distance. "I was afraid you'd both gone under, and if you had I'd never have forgiven myself for taking you up with me."

"We were just starting out to look for you," said Frank. "Where did you land?"

"In a good soft place," said the other. "The branches of a big tree. My ankle caught in a branch and got wrenched a little, but otherwise I'm O.K."

"I landed in the river, and Frank had to fish me out," said Bart. "But now that we're all safe, I'm beginning to wonder just where we are. The storm seems to be over, and I guess it's up to us to get back to camp as soon as possible, or they'll have us down as A.W.O.L."

"I'm not sure just where we are," responded Dunton, "but I hope we haven't landed among the Huns. They'd like nothing better than a chance to put us out of the way."

"Well, all we've got to do to get back is follow the river down," said Frank. "Let's go."

Following Frank's suggestion, they had not gone more than half a mile when, to their great satisfaction, they caught sight of an American sentry walking his post.

"Good!" exclaimed Dunton. "That means that we're still in the occupied zone. We'll just ask this bird where we are."

Inquiring of the sentry, they learned that they had landed at Montabaur, which was on the very edge of the zone occupied by the American Army. The sentry gave them directions as to the best way to reach camp. They arrived there without further mishap, and separated, the two friends hastening to their barracks, and Dunton to his headquarters to make a report on the loss of the balloon.

Great was the joy of Tom and Billy at seeing their comrades safe and sound, as they had been under intense anxiety concerning them.

"But we might have known better than to have worried about you," said Billy finally, after he and Tom had heard the story of their adventure. "I had a hunch all along that you'd both come piking along sometime to-night or to-morrow, and after this, I refuse to worry in any degree about you. It serves you right, anyway, for going up without us."

"Well, in the future, you can go up without me all you want to," laughed Frank. "How about it, Bart?"

"You said it," acquiesced Bart heartily. "I'm off that parachute stuff for all time. I know when I've had enough, and this is one of the times."

"The way it looks around here," said Billy soberly, "it isn't going to be necessary to go up in the air to find excitement. All the evening we've been hearing reports of big riots going on in Coblenz, and everybody says we're likely to be called out to-morrow to do a little suppressing act."

CHAPTER XIII

GERMAN RIOTING

For once rumor had not overstated things. The most turbulent rioting the city had ever seen started the next day, and, in spite of all the efforts of the authorities, seemed to increase in intensity as the day wore on. The German authorities seemed to be utterly helpless to cope with the situation, and finally the American troops had to be called upon to quell the disturbances.

"What did I tell you?" exclaimed Billy, when the order came through to get under arms. "We're in for a nice little shindy now, as sure as guns. But as far as I'm concerned, I'm glad of a chance to teach these Huns how to behave. The trouble with us is, we're entirely too easy with them."

"Yes, we're not half as strict as we ought to be," assented Frank. "But the more monkey business they try, the tighter the lid is going to be clamped down, as they'll find to their cost."

But in point of fact, the rioting was not so much against the American authorities as it was against the German authorities who were operating under the protection and direction of the Americans.

But it was all one to the boys, as all they cared about was the prospect of some pleasurable excitement. And more excitement was brewing for them than they anticipated, for this was by far the most serious riot that had occurred since they had entered German territory, and was one not easily to be suppressed.

The regiment was not long in getting ready, and was soon swinging out of camp, headed toward the rebellious city. As the soldiers approached it, they could hear the sound of rifle firing, mingled with the sharper sound of machine gun fire.

"Something doing, all right," said Bart, as they swung rapidly along. "Sounds as though some one were getting trouble, and plenty of it, and I'm willing to bet the Heinies are getting the worst end of it."

"You can bet they are," agreed Billy. "And just wait till this bunch of bad men gets after them. It begins to seem like old times again."

"Right you are," said Tom. "And whatever's going to happen, it will be pretty soon, because we're getting close."

By this time they were indeed on the outskirts of the town, and before long were swinging down one of the main streets, the noise of rifle firing and shouting growing steadily louder as they progressed. At first few people were to be seen, although here and there an anxious face peered out of an upper window.

But as they penetrated further into the heart of the city, they encountered hurrying and shouting knots of men, who, however, hastily changed their direction when they caught sight of the businesslike appearance of the Americans.

Homer Randall

Suddenly Billy caught sight of a face at an upper window that seemed familiar.

"There's the fellow that tried to strike the lame man the day you took his cane away from him, Frank!" he exclaimed.

Frank looked in the direction that Billy indicated just as the man was hastily withdrawing behind a curtain.

"Couldn't see much of him, but it did look something like him," he remarked. "But I shouldn't be surprised to find him mixed up in this trouble. He's the kind that would be in the thick of it."

Just then there was a flash from the window and a bullet whizzed by the Army Boys and flattened against the wall on the other side of the street.

"I'll bet that was aimed at you, Frank!" exclaimed Bart. "That fellow's a bad shot but he has a good memory."

The shot was quickly followed by others from windows and roofs, but fortunately, the snipers were in too much of a hurry to take effective aim, and their bullets did little damage at first.

But as the Americans marched on, they encountered constantly increasing opposition. Several of the soldiers had been wounded by the time they had reached the thick of the disturbance. When they turned a corner into one of the main streets of the town they found that a barricade had been erected across it, and this barricade was being held by a small force of Americans, who, hemmed in on every side by Germans, were finding it a hard task to hold out against tremendously heavy odds. But the advent of reinforcements turned the tide of battle for the time being, and the mob quickly took to its heels and left the Americans a brief breathing space.

The new arrivals were welcomed lustily, and soon found themselves within the barricades, where they commenced a brisk fire against their unseen enemies on roof and at window, who still kept up a scattering fire. Meanwhile, the leaders held a brief consultation to decide their immediate course of action.

It was decided to dispatch small bodies of men, as many as could be spared, to clean up the adjacent streets, and so prevent the rioters from massing again.

The four Army Boys, together with twelve of their company, two squads in all, found themselves detailed to a narrow street, and they soon found that their task was going to prove no sinecure. The street was very narrow, bordered by tall, peaked houses, and every house seemed to shelter two or three riflemen. It was only occasionally that the Americans could see their opponents, but when a German did venture to expose himself for a moment, his slip almost invariably proved fatal, as the American rifles spoke with deadly effect. But the Americans were at a terrible disadvantage, and the sergeant in charge saw this and acted accordingly.

"Break up into groups," he ordered, "part on one side of the street and part on the other, and go from house to house. Clean them out thoroughly, and show no mercy to anybody you find with a rifle in his hand. We'll assemble again at the end of this street."

This plan was put into immediate operation. The four Army Boys were together. With their rifle butts they battered in the doors of houses, then fought their way up to the roofs against the most treacherous opposition. Again and again one or the other escaped death by what seemed a miracle, and they saw to it that the Huns paid the price for these attacks. The second house that they entered was a large one, and seemed a veritable maze of rooms, for each one of which they had to fight to gain possession. As they reached the foot of the stairway leading up to the top story, they saw three burly Germans at the top, rifles in hand, evidently prepared to stop the hated Americans at any cost.

"Surrender!" shouted Frank.

For answer, one of the Germans, who appeared to be the leader, leveled his rifle at Frank's head, but before he could pull the trigger, Bart's big automatic pistol spoke once, and the German swayed, stumbled, and came crashing down the staircase.

"Now's the time, fellows!" yelled Frank, as he saw the remaining two Germans hesitate after the fall of their leader. "Let's get 'em and get 'em quick! Treat them rough!" As he spoke all the boys leaped up the staircase, firing as they mounted.

But before they could reach the top reinforcements arrived for the Huns in the shape of three others of their countrymen. Nothing daunted, the Army Boys rushed on. As they fired one German fell, but the others presented a determined front, although their aim was bad, and so far none of the boys had been seriously wounded, although both Tom and Frank had been grazed by flying bullets. In a few more steps they were among the Germans, and then ensued a fierce hand to hand fight on the narrow landing. The Germans proved themselves no mean antagonists, and for a few minutes there was a wild medley of blows and shouts. The boys fought desperately, and slowly forced their antagonists back against a light balustrade that guarded the stair well.

Suddenly there was a sharp snapping sound, the frail railing gave way, and with wild shouts and oaths the Germans hurtled over the edge for a sheer drop of three stories.

So suddenly did this happen, that the boys had the greatest difficulty in preventing themselves from following, but they recovered in time, and peered over. Three of their late enemies lay still as they had fallen, but the fourth showed some signs of life.

"Whew!" ejaculated Frank, wiping the sweat from his eyes, "we had it hot and heavy here for a time, didn't we?"

"I should say we did!" exclaimed Bart. "But that railing was a good friend to us. I hate Germans, but I've got to admit that those birds knew the rudiments of close-in fighting."

"Well, they're done for now," said Billy, "and it looks as though we had cleaned this house up pretty thoroughly. If we have this much trouble in every house we tackle, I can see where we've got our work cut out for us."

"I think maybe it would be better to go up to the top of this house," said Frank, and then enter the adjoining one from the roof. Anybody in it will be expecting an attack from the street, and going in that way we may be able to take them by surprise."

"That's a good idea" exclaimed Bart. "Lead on, old timer."

Frank's plan proved to be a good one. They met with no further opposition while mounting to the roof, and once there, they located the scuttle leading into the next house. Fortunately this was not fastened, those in the house probably having left it unlocked with the idea in mind of facilitating their own escape.

As Frank Sheldon deduced, they had not considered the possibility of an attack from above.

Opening the trap door, the four friends descended the short length of ladder that led perpendicularly downward. So far they had heard no sound to apprise them of the presence of a lurking enemy, and they began to think that possibly the house was deserted. Then stopping and listening intently, they heard the muffled sound of voices, apparently coming from the floor below.

Here was something of a problem presented to the boys, for they had no orders, nor indeed, desire, to molest those peaceably inclined, and were only after revolutionists and rioters who were doing the sniping work. But their doubts were soon set at rest. From the front of the house came the sharp sound of rifle firing, and the boys hastened in that direction. On the second floor they burst into the large front room, taking completely by surprise a group of some four or five men who were sulking in the shelter of the windows. As the boys burst into the room they whirled about, only to find themselves looking into the muzzles of four vicious looking army pistols.

"Drop those guns and put up your hands," commanded Frank. All obeyed but one man, who raised his rifle to his shoulder. Before he could pull the trigger a spurt of fire flashed from Frank's pistol, and the man sagged slowly to the floor.

"Downstairs with the rest of you!" ordered Frank, at the same time motioning toward the stairway. "We can't do much with these men except disarm them," he said in an aside to his companions, as the Germans sullenly prepared to obey. "We've got to clean out this house and a lot of others, and we haven't got enough men to guard prisoners. You break up their rifles, Tom, and then rejoin us in the street."

They herded the Germans downstairs, and at the street entrance propelled them forth with a few hearty kicks. This pleasurable duty had hardly been performed when they were rejoined by Tom, who had smashed the German rifles over the window sills, putting them very effectively out of commission.

Meanwhile, the other parties had been doing good work, and the sniping had to a great extent died down. The boys entered the next house, but met with no opposition, and when they reached the top story an open scuttle giving on to the roof told its own story of flight on the part of the occupants. They went through several houses in this fashion, but when they neared the end of the block resistance began to stiffen. Across the end of the street was a house that commanded it absolutely, and this seemed to have been chosen by the rioters as a last stand. From every window and from the roof snipers were busy, and were inflicting serious damage on the Americans. Already three had been killed, and as many more wounded. The sergeant marshaled the slender force remaining to him.

"Boys," he said, "we've got to clean out that hornet's nest, and then I think we'll have things pretty much in our own hands. We'll rush it now, and be sure that every man hangs close to the others, because if we become separated we're done for. Now, all together, and let them have it plenty!"

With these the little force of intrepid Americans rushed for the door of this last remaining stronghold. The door was of course locked, but when half a dozen vigorous young Americans charged it like so many battering rams, it gave way, and the soldiers surged forward into a large hallway. A wide staircase led upward from one side of this hall, and from an upper landing a spiteful rain of bullets zipped about the Americans. One fell, but the others, led by the big sergeant, rushed up the staircase, emptying their pistols as they went. The resistance met here was the most solid they had encountered that day, and they soon found that they had their work cut out for them.

When they reached the landing and engaged in hand to hand work with the Germans, other doors giving on the landing opened, and more rioters appeared to give aid to their companions. For a time the fight seemed to be in favor of the Germans, as their number told, and then in favor of the Americans, who had the advantage of discipline and team work on their side. Two more of their number had fallen, however, and the remaining Americans fought with the fury of desperation added to their usual dauntless courage. They took merciless toll of German lives, and at last the rioters, astonished and dismayed at their own losses, began to give way. Suddenly they were seized by panic, and to a man turned and fled through a long hall that ran the length of the house.

"Keep after them, boys," panted Sergeant Dan. "Don't give them a chance to recover themselves. We've got 'em on the run now, and we want to keep 'em that way."

The Americans followed the rioters down the passageway, reloading their weapons as they ran. At the end of the hall a sharp turn gave access to another stairway, and up this the Germans rushed in headlong flight, the Americans close on their heels. Another and last flight of stairs took them up to the roof, and this once reached, they broke and ran in every direction, some disappearing through the roof-scuttles of adjoining buildings, and others hiding behind chimneys and other roof structures.

The Americans paused for breath and consultation, and Sergeant Dan walked to the edge of the roof nearest the street and peered over.

"Guess our job's done for the present," he said, when he returned to his command. "Everything seems quiet in the street below, and there's not a soul in sight. Now let's take stock of damages, and then we'll hike back to the rendezvous."

As the soldiers were taking stock of each other, a sudden fear gripped at Frank's heart, and he exclaimed:

"Tom! Where's Tom?"

Billy and Bart gazed at him and at each other in dismay.

"He was with us when we attacked this house," said Billy. "I remember he was right alongside of me when we bumped that door, and we landed on the floor together when it gave way. But that's the last I remember of seeing him."

Neither of the others had any later recollection of their friend's presence.

"He may be downstairs wounded," said Frank. "Come on, fellows, we've got to find him," and forgetful of military discipline in their anxiety over their friend, the three comrades dashed through the door leading into the building.

"We'll all go down," said the sergeant. "Some of our fellows have taken the last count, but others are only wounded, and we want to get them to a hospital just as soon as we can."

Frank, Bart, and Billy made a frantic search of the building, but found no trace of their missing friend.

"He may have been badly wounded but have been able to make his way to the street where he would be picked up and taken to a hospital," speculated Frank. "Or it's possible that he has been captured," he added. "As soon as we have reported back to headquarters with our detachment, we'll try to get permission to make a search of the hospitals and see if we can't find him there."

There was little else they could do, so with heavy hearts they rejoined their companions who had rigged rude stretchers for two of their wounded comrades and were making ready to march back to headquarters.

The sergeant knew of the attachment existing between the four friends, and sympathized with the grief of the three remaining over the loss of their comrade.

"The chances are," he said, "that Bradford has been captured by the rioters, and the military police will find out where he is and get hold of him. Remember that an American soldier takes a lot of killing before he's actually dead."

But the boys marched in gloomy silence, and their hearts were sad for their friend.

The rioting had been effectually quelled, and the streets were once more quiet. The little party soon reached their head-quarters, where the sergeant made his report. The boys could hardly control their impatience until the time came when they were off duty. They immediately secured permission to make inquiries at the hospitals which were taking care of the casualties sustained during the rioting. There were three of these, and each of the boys went to a different one, agreeing to meet in a designated place as soon as they had completed their inquiries. An hour later they assembled as they had agreed, only to learn that so far their search had been fruitless.

"The only thing left for us to do," said Frank, "is to go back to the barracks, where maybe by this time they will have posted a list of the casualties. If Tom's name is not there well be pretty sure that he's been captured, and it will be up to us to try to find him."

Returning to the barracks as Frank had proposed, they found that a list was posted on the company bulletin board, and carefully scanned it for Tom's name, while fear tugged at their hearts.

Great was their relief when they failed to find it, for if he were only a prisoner the chances were that the authorities would get him back, or that the boys themselves might ferret out the place where he was being held and rescue him.

"Well," said Bart, as the boys turned away from the bulletin board, "there's not much we can do for poor Tom to-night, but if he's a prisoner we'll get word from him sooner or later."

"If he's a prisoner, I'd hate to be the man who has him in charge," remarked Billy grimly. "Something pretty terrible is apt to happen to that bird most any time."

"Yes, chances are he'll come marching into camp with a few prisoners on his own account." said Frank. "That is, if he doesn't catch this new disease they're talking about,"

"What disease?" asked Billy. "I hadn't heard anything about it."

"Nobody seems to know very much about it," replied Frank. "It has appeared at various places in Germany, especially in the occupied zones. It seems to have attacked Germans as well as Americans, and nobody knows what to make of it. Of course, remember I'm only telling you what another fellow told me recently, and I give it to you for what it's worth. It may be just rumor, but he seemed to be so certain of his facts that I felt inclined to believe him."

As it happened, what Frank had heard as a rumor was indeed a fact—and a fact, moreover, that was proving most puzzling and unpleasant for the American medical authorities. The disease that Frank had spoken of had indeed made its appearance in various parts of the country, and while the doctors had many theories concerning it, they were all only theories as yet, and nothing really definite was known regarding it. The symptoms were much like those of virulent typhus. Men sickened and died within forty- eight hours, and once stricken, the unfortunate victim did not recover in one case out of a hundred.

Some of the doctors were inclined to think it one of the plagues that usually follow in the track of war, due to privation and depression. This theory, however, did not explain why American troops, well fed and victorious, should be affected. Most believed it to be caused by some deadly germ, hitherto unknown, and every effort was being made by the medical corps to isolate the germ and find a remedy for the disease. But the Army Boys were to know more of the source of this strange scourge and make a most amazing discovery regarding it.

CHAPTER XIV

ON THE TRAIL

On the day following that of Tom Bradford's disappearance, Bart and Billy were assigned to special duty as part of an officers' escort on a mission to a neighboring town.

After they had left Frank found himself very lonely, especially as he had an afternoon off duty. Mingled with his thoughts of the missing Tom was the thought that had constantly haunted his mind of late—the unsolved mystery of the alley up which hostile Germans could flit and apparently disappear into thin air. He knew there must be some explanation of the mystery, but what was it? He racked his brains to find a plausible solution. But the more he thought about it, the more uncertain he became, until at last he came to a resolution.

"Here I am," he thought, "racking my wits over this matter, and about all I do is just guess work, after all. The best thing I can do is get permission to go to the town, find that alley and see if I can't run across some clue that was lacking the last time I was there."

Having reached this resolve, he lost no time in acting on it, and readily securing the desired permission, he set off for the

Homer Randall

town. This he soon reached, and walked at a smart pace through the quaint, well-kept streets.

Going along one broad avenue he came suddenly face to face with the man from whom he had taken away the cane, whom he had since learned was a famous German physician, a well known character throughout the war. The latter, however, was so preoccupied that he took no notice of Frank. His thoughts, whatever they were, appeared to be pleasant, for as he walked he smiled to himself and softly rubbed his hands together, as one well pleased with the course of events.

"The old codger seems mightily pleased over something," mused Frank, "and I'm willing to bet a reasonable amount it isn't over any schemes for the betterment of mankind. I may do him an injustice, but I don't think his genial Hun nature is inclined exactly in that direction."

He gave little further thought to the chance meeting, his mind being busied with speculations as to what he might find in the mysterious alley. The weather was very mild, and he knew the sheet of ice and snow that had covered the ground on his previous visit would not now exist to baffle him. But he did not want to enter the alley until darkness had fallen to offer him concealment, so abated his usual brisk pace to a mere saunter, and took careful note of the attitude of the people he passed. The streets were quiet enough, but the faces of the inhabitants were sullen and hostile, and Frank could read enmity in the glances cast at him.

"They love the Americans about as much as they love sunstroke," he meditated. "But it doesn't matter much what they like, because they'll take just what's handed to them. But it's the lower elements and the revolutionists who are making most of the trouble, and I'm a lot mistaken if their headquarters aren't in the neighborhood of that blind alley.

Well, anyway, I'll know more about it when I get through my privately conducted explorations this evening."

He stopped in a small restaurant and ordered a light meal. By the time he had finished this it was nearly dark, and he set out for his objective without further delay.

He shortly reached the entrance to the alley, and, after casting a searching glance about him to make sure that he was unobserved, he slipped cautiously into the place.

"It ought to be a lot easier for me to locate that trap door now than it was when I was here with Bart," he thought. "There's no ice now, and if there is a door, I'll be bound to find it."

He proceeded cautiously up the alley, taking every precaution to avoid noise, and soon reached the blank wall that had so baffled him and his friends on a previous occasion. He drew a flashlight from his pocket, and when he thought he was close to the place where he and Bart had previously located the door he cautiously played the tiny spot of light over the ground. At first he thought he must be mistaken, as this part of the alley seemed to be like all the rest. But, looking closer, his heart leaped as he made out the outline of a heavy iron ring, lying flat in a recess in the pavement, and almost covered with gravel and dust. So cunningly was it concealed that it would inevitably have escaped observation unless one were actually looking for it.

"There's a trap door here, all right," he exulted. "Now, I wonder if I can get in, or if it will be fastened from the inside. Here goes to find out."

With the thought, he worked the iron ring loose from the dirt, set himself for the effort, and gave a tentative tug. The door did not give a particle, and he tried again, this time putting every ounce of his strength into the effort. The door gave a little, but with all his strength Frank could not lift it more than an inch or two. He tried again and again, but with no better result, and at last, to his great disappointment he was forced to give over the attempt for the time being.

"Guess this is more than a one-man job," he thought to himself. "What I'll have to do is to bring Bart and Billy here to-morrow night, and I think the three of us can lift the door easily. I've made one big step, anyway, for now I know there is really a trap door here, and before we weren't sure of it."

He pressed the iron ring down into its socket, scattered some earth and gravel over it, and at last satisfied that he had left everything as he had found it and in such a condition as not to arouse suspicion if the secret entrance was used by one of the plotters before he could return, he turned his footsteps toward camp.

CHAPTER XV

A BARE CHANCE

Frank was now convinced that he and his comrades had really chanced on a big secret, and he was eager to get them and get to the heart of the matter. He was greatly disappointed that he had been unable to follow up the adventure that very evening, but with a soldier's philosophy promised himself better luck the next time, and swung off toward camp with a stride that soon brought him to his destination.

But the Army Boy's plan for an immediate further investigation of the mysterious alley was destined to have a further setback, for the next day great aeroplane activity started all over the American front, and it was announced that nobody would be given leave to visit Coblenz until further notice. It seemed that reports had been received at general headquarters that the rioters, driven out of Coblenz, were gathering in smaller towns throughout the occupied area, and making demonstrations and inflammatory speeches against the American "invaders."

Many aviators were detailed to fly over all the neighboring territory and get information of the movements and numbers of the rioters, so that troops could be sent to the threatened points and suppress the uprisings before they assumed serious proportions.

Among the aviators detailed to this work was Dick Lever, and on his return from one of these excursions he sought out his Army Boy friends. For a considerable time he had been detailed to other parts of the occupied territory, but now his headquarters were temporarily near the barracks in which the boys were situated.

So it happened that one evening as Frank, Bart, and Billy were strolling toward the canteen, they were both surprised and delighted to espy the long, athletic figure of their friend. Dick was no less glad to see them, and everybody for some distance around was apprised of the fact that old comrades had met once more.

"But where's Tom?" inquired Dick, after the first burst of enthusiasm was over. "I'm so used to seeing you fellows as a quartette that your sweet voices don't sound exactly correct as a trio."

The faces of all the boys lengthened at this allusion to their missing friend, and in a few words they explained to Dick the circumstances of his sudden disappearance.

"By Jove!" exclaimed Dick excitedly, when they had finished, "I wouldn't be a bit surprised if I could put you on his trail."

"What do you mean?" chorused the boys.

"Now, don't get excited," said Dick. "What I'm going to tell you may not be of the least importance after all. It's just this. While I was reconnoitering over the various camps of the revolutionists, in one of them I was sure I saw a man in an

American Army uniform. I was too far up to recognize him even if I had known him, and it might be any American prisoner other than Tom, or it might be a German dressed in an American uniform for spying purposes. Anyway, if I hadn't been under special rush orders to return as soon as possible, I would have gone down and maybe attempted a rescue, but I had to get back immediately with my information, so couldn't take any chances."

"But can you give us any idea of the direction of the camp where you saw this man?" inquired Frank. "If we had the least idea where to look for him, you can bet we'd get him away from those renegade Germans, and likely hurt anybody that got in the way, too."

"I'd hate to be the obstacle, myself," grinned Dick. "But, to get down to business, I can give you a rough idea of the direction and distance, and in addition, I guess I don't have to tell you that if there's anything I can do to help, you can count on me to the limit."

The three boys and Dick shook hands all around as they accepted this offer, and on the spot organized as a committee of ways and means to rescue their missing comrade. Dick could only tell them approximately where he had seen the man in American uniform, and the Spartacides changed their camps so often in order to escape detection and capture that even this information was of rather doubtful value.

"The best thing I can suggest is this," said Dick, at last. "I've been detailed to try out some new aeroplanes to-morrow, and as long as I take them up and fly them, it doesn't much matter what direction I go in, provided I don't go too far. Now, what's to prevent me from flying a few miles in the direction I last saw this particular bunch of revolutionists, and taking a chance on finding out something more?"

"We'll appreciate anything you can do in that direction," said Frank. "You've given us a clue now, at any rate, and you can bet we won't be slow in following it up. It's going to be some problem to get hold of him, but we've solved as hard ones before now, and I guess we won't let this stump us."

"You told it!" said Bart emphatically. "If the Germans couldn't get one of us while the war was on, it's a cinch they won't be able to now when it's all over. If old Tom's alive, we'll rescue him some way."

Dick Lever described the location of the Spartacides' camp with as much exactness as he could, and even drew a rough map of the surrounding country, marking the place where he had seen the American prisoner with a cross.

The boys thanked him heartily, and then walked back to his section of the camp, as it was getting close to the time for taps, and Dick had to be back at his quarters by then. On the way they talked over old times, and Dick promised to visit them again at the first opportunity, and made them promise once more to call on him for help if they thought he could be of service in rescuing Tom. Then they all shook hands, and Bart, Frank, and Billy hurried back to their own quarters, full of excitement over the news that Dick had brought them and hopes that they would soon have Tom with them again.

But this was not to prove quite as quickly nor easily done as they had anticipated, for conditions were so disturbed that small detachments were not permitted to go into the surrounding country lest they should be attacked and overwhelmed by superior forces that might bear them down by sheer force of numbers.

They had to abandon therefore the plan to hunt Tom unaided, and Frank went direct to his lieutenant and told him just what they had learned from Dick regarding the presence of an American prisoner in the Spartacides' hands and their suspicion that it might possibly be their missing comrade.

To his surprise, he learned that the lieutenant had already received a report from other sources that tallied closely with Dick's. It was intolerable that any American should be left a prisoner in the hands of desperate men who might at any moment take his life, and plans were maturing to descend on the place where he was believed to be held. An adequate force would be provided and would set out as soon as possible.

With an inward prayer that the attempt would be made soon, Frank left the lieutenant's presence and hurried away to tell the good news to Billy and Bart.

CHAPTER XVI

RAISING THE TRAP DOOR

"I hear that a detachment is getting ready to go over to look into that matter of the prisoner that Dick told us about," said Frank Sheldon, a little later when he and his comrades were coming out from mess.

"I hope we're slated to go along with it," said Billy eagerly.

"Here comes the corp," remarked Bart. "Let's ask him. He'll probably be in charge of it."

As Corporal Wilson approached, the boys intercepted him.

"I can guess what you're going to ask," he said with a smile; "and I'll answer it right now. Yes, you fellows are going with the detachment. Plans are making now, but there's so much doing right here just now that we won't be able to start until to-morrow."

"To-morrow?" repeated Frank in disappointment, and his feeling was mirrored on the faces of his companions.

"Sorry," said Wilson as he passed along, "but orders are orders, and we can't get off any sooner."

"And who knows what may happen to Tom in the meantime?" said Billy sorrowfully.

"It's exasperating," said Frank. "It makes me crazy to think of another twenty-four hours going by while we're doing nothing to help him."

"The only comfort is the confidence I have in Tom's luck," said Bart "That boy sure must have a rabbit's foot around him somewhere. He has as many lives as a cat. Do you remember how he got away from that drunken German bunch that had a rope all ready to hang him? And the slick way he got away in a barrel from the prison camp? I tell you that the bullet isn't molded that will kill that boy, and don't you forget it."

"I only hope you're right," returned Frank. "All the same I'll feel a whole lot easier in my mind when the old scout is with us again."

Just then a litter passed them carrying a sick man to the hospital ward.

"Those things are getting a little too common to suit me," remarked Frank. "The health of the boys here used to be fine. Now they say that the hospitals are getting overcrowded."

"And a good many of those who go in aren't coming out again, that's the worst of it," observed Billy. "That cemetery on the hill is getting altogether too full."

"If this mysterious disease isn't checked it will be worse than the 'flu,'" said Bart. "What's the matter with our doctors anyway? Why don't they get on the job?"

"You can't blame them," Frank defended. "There's no better

medical staff in any army than the one we've got. They're working like mad to try to isolate the germ, or whatever it is, that's causing this mysterious trouble. But they seem to be all at sea in this matter. It's an entirely new thing, and they haven't found any way to conquer it."

"It would be rather hard luck to come through St. Mihiel and the Argonne, and then to be knocked out by a measly disease like this," said Billy disgustedly.

"Well, it hasn't got us yet, and let's hope it won't," said Frank. "But now that we've got a chance, what do you fellows say if we go over tonight and try to get at the bottom of that alley mystery? I shan't be easy in my mind until I've solved it."

"Always looking for trouble," laughed Bart. "But I don't mind confessing that the matter's got tight hold of me too, and I'm game to see it through to a finish."

"Count me in," said Billy.

"If only poor Tom were with us!" mourned Frank "It's just the kind of thing he'd like to trail. And if there should happen to be any scrapping, he'd be a mighty handy lad to have along with us. He'd rather fight than eat any time."

After the drills and work of the day were over they got permission to go to the town and started across the river just as twilight was falling.

While passing through one of the streets, they met the famous German physician, from whom they customarily got a look that betrayed his hate of the American uniform. But this time, to their surprise, he was rubbing his hands and seemed to be in high good humor.

"What's come over his nibs, I wonder," remarked Billy. "Usually he seems to have a grouch of the worst kind, but to look at him now you might think that he'd just had news of a good fat legacy."

"He is different, for a fact." agreed Bart. "He couldn't look happier if Germany had won the war."

They looked after him, and saw him vanishing into the doorway of a dwelling that was really a mansion.

"Swell place that," observed Billy. "He must have a peach of a practice to live in a house like that."

"He's one of the most famous men in his line in Germany I've heard," commented Frank.

"They say the Kaiser himself used to consult him. But of late they say that he's made himself almost a hermit. Seems that he's given up his regular practice, and simply nurses his grouch because Germany was licked."

"He sits up pretty late to do it then," put in Billy. "I've been on sentry duty in this street, and many a time I've seen a light in his office until almost morning."

"Here's our corner," Frank said, as they came to the next street.

They approached the alley with the utmost caution, and slipped into its darkness when they felt sure that they were unobserved.

"That's queer!" exclaimed Frank, gazing above the blank wall at the outline of a tall building that rose beyond it.

"What's queer?" asked Billy.

"Why, that building there is the same one the doctor went into," answered his companion. "I know it by that cupola on the top. It must back up right against this wall. In fact, this wall is part of the rear wall of the house. I thought these were only factories."

"Oh, well, what if it is?" returned Bart. "We'd better get busy here before we're interrupted. Let's hope there isn't another fire in this district to-night."

Without much difficulty they found the square place that Frank and Bart had noticed on their previous visit. They scraped away the ice and gravel and discovered the ring by which the trap door was evidently raised. Then they braced themselves and gave a mighty tug.

But the effort was unavailing. They were far stronger than the ordinary run of men, and yet even their trained muscles had to confess defeat.

"Perhaps it's locked or bolted on the other side," suggested Bart.

"Not likely," answered Frank. "It's more probable that it's frozen in. Get out your knives and dig around the edge of the door, and then we'll try again."

They did this for perhaps five minutes, and then tried again.

This time the door moved but did not yield. Once more they bent their backs to the work, and this time they won. Slowly and creakingly the door rose, showing a yawning chasm beneath, while a rush of fetid air assailed their nostrils!

CHAPTER XVII

A PERILOUS SITUATION

The three Army Boys started back almost letting go the trap door in their desire to escape the noxious odor and fill their lungs with the cool winter air.

"What is this anyway—the entrance to the infernal regions?" asked Billy.

"If it were, it couldn't smell much worse, I imagine," answered Bart.

"We're not going to let a thing like that hold us back, are we?" asked Frank impatiently.

"Of course not," replied Billy. "But that doesn't say we have to like it, does it? Flash that light of yours and let us see just what this sweet smelling thing looks like."

Frank directed the rays of his flashlight into the gloomy recess, and the light fell on a small platform about four feet below the level of the ground. Two or three stone steps descended from this and then they could faintly see a rough stone floor from which several passages branched out in different directions.

He returned the light to his pocket, and the three held a whispered conversation.

"Well, fellows, you've seen as much of it as I have," said Frank. "What do you say? Shall we explore it?"

"Sure thing," replied Bart. "What do you think we are, a bunch of four flushers?"

"Lead on, old scout," said Billy. "But first we must wedge this door up a trifle, so as to be able to open it easily when we come back."

"Right you are!" said Frank. "When we do come back we may have to come in a hurry for all we know, and we want to be able to lift this up in a jiffy."

They hunted around until they found a small slab of stone which they wedged under the door, after they had dropped down into the space below. Then, with Frank in the van, with his flashlight sending its rays ahead of them, they ventured slowly into the unknown, feeling their way with the utmost caution.

The stone floor was uneven and damp, and at times they stepped into pools of noisome water that was covered with green scum. The sides of the narrow passages were covered with mold, and the air was heavy and offensive.

Suddenly Frank stepped back with a sharp exclamation, and at the same instant there was a squeal, and a gray form scurried away into the darkness.

"A rat!" he murmured to his friends behind him. "I stepped fairly on him. A mighty big fellow he was, too."

They went on a little further, keeping close together, for there were several passages that branched off from what seemed to be the main one, and if they became separated it might be difficult for them to get together again, especially as Frank was the only one of the trio who had a flashlight.

And now their ears were assailed by soft patterings and shufflings that seemed to increase in number as they progressed. Their eyes caught certain red points that flared like sparks and then vanished, only to reappear. It was as though a host of eerie things were keeping tab on their movements, and after a while this silent mustering of unseen watchers got on their nerves.

Billy, who came last, was passing one of the passages that branched off to the left when he thought he caught a glimpse of light. He went into this side passage for a few steps to make sure, and verified his first impression. There, sure enough, was an electric bulb, on the opposite side of which he could see the outline of a door.

He was hurrying back to tell his comrades what he had seen when he heard an exclamation from Bart that quickened his steps still more. Bart's right hand was holding on to his left, and in the light that Frank had directed on it he saw that the hand was bleeding.

"It was a rat," Bart exclaimed wrathfully, as he nursed his wounded hand. "The beggar jumped straight at it. It feels as though he'd made his teeth meet through it"

Billy whipped out his handkerchief and was binding it around his comrade's hand, when a gray form sprang from the darkness and fastened its teeth in his trousers leg just grazing the skin. Frank made a kick at it, but as he did so, his foot slipped on the damp stone and the flashlight flew out of his hand, leaving them in utter darkness. He stooped to try to find it, but his hand touched a furry coat and he drew back just in time to escape a savage snap.

Then as if by magic those red pin points, that they now knew were eyes, seemed to spring up from every direction. There were rats everywhere, an army of them, rats ahead of them and rats behind them, gathering to oust these human intruders from their domain. Singly they were contemptible opponents, but now they had the strength that came from numbers, and they knew it.

And the Army Boys knew it too. For an instant panic gripped at their hearts. The next moment they had pulled themselves together.

"Back to the trap door, fellows!" said Frank tensely. "Fast, but not too fast. Don't run. And don't shoot, or we may hit each other. Draw your revolvers and club them off with the butts."

They retraced their steps as well as they could in the darkness. The rats knew that they were retreating, and they grew bolder. Again and again they fastened themselves on their arms and legs, and had to be beaten off with the revolver butts. All the boys were bitten many times, and it seemed to them that they would never come to the end of the passage alive. But none of their assailants reached their throats, although one had to be knocked from Billy's shoulder, and at last the nightmare journey ended when they stumbled against the steps that led to the trap door. Frantically they heaved the door up and clambered out and sank down on the ice covered ground, spent and out of breath and utterly exhausted.

CHAPTER XVIII

THE CRITICAL MOMENT

For a time the Army Boys sat there, panting and gasping from their unwonted exertions, yet filled with a deep thankfulness that they had won through as well as they had.

At length Frank gave a short laugh that had in it little trace of mirth.

"Three husky doughboys of the American Army put to flight by a horde of rats!" he exclaimed.

"All the same, they'd be picking the bones of those same husky doughboys if we hadn't vamoosed," defended Billy. "Gee! it seemed to me that there must have been millions of them."

"I know now how that Bishop Hatto, or whoever it was, felt when the rats were after him," put in Bart. "If we'd only had some clubs with us we might have had a chance."

"Well, they made us show our backs, and that's something the Huns were never able to do," said Frank. "But I guess we'd better get back to the barracks and cauterize these bites. I don't know how you fellows made out, but I'll bet they bit me in twenty places. I'm bleeding fiercely."

"Same here," echoed Billy.

"I feel as though I were one big wound," said Bart lugubriously. "But say, fellows, don't let on what we've been up against or the boys will guy us to death."

"And to think we've been to all this trouble only to find that we'd stumbled into a sewer," said Frank disgustedly. "That's what it must have been, guessing by the smell."

"Oh by the way!" exclaimed Billy, as a thought struck him. "I meant to tell you fellows, but the fight with the rats put it out of my mind. There was an electric light in one of those passages."

Frank, who had gotten to his feet and started to walk away, stopped as though he had been shot.

"What's that?" he demanded sharply.

"Fact," replied Billy. "I could see it plainly, and behind it I saw the outline of a door. I started to tell you fellows about it, and then I heard one of you shout and I didn't think of the thing again till this blessed minute."

"Well, that certainly was hard luck!" exclaimed Frank bitterly. "Ten to one that's the clue to the mystery. My hunch wasn't a false alarm after all. I've a good mind to go back right now and finish the job."

"Not on your life you won't!" said Bart decidedly. "Not if Billy and I have to hold you back by main force. Why, boy, you're crazy. Those rats have tasted blood, and they're full of fight. And then, too, we haven't any clubs to beat them off. It would be sheer suicide to go in there again to-night."

"Bart is right," acquiesced Billy. "Some other night perhaps when we're in shape for it, but not now. Come along, old man, and use your common sense."

Frank knew in his heart that his friends were right, but it galled him horribly to defer the adventure.

"Well," he agreed reluctantly, "we'll call it a night's work and let it go at that. But I'm only giving it on the promise that we'll try it again. We've never let anything in Hunland get away with us yet, and it's too late to start it now. If I live I'm going to get to the bottom of this."

"Sure thing," agreed Bart. "We're just as keen to clear it up as you are. But this isn't our lucky night. Let's light out for the barracks and fix up these bites."

They made their way back and slipped in as unobtrusively as they could, and after they had cauterized and dressed their wounds they sought to forget their disappointment in sleep.

The next day found them stiff and sore, but this feeling wore off as the day progressed, and when night came they forgot everything in their eagerness to be on the march to hunt for their missing comrade, who had hardly for a moment been out of their thoughts.

The plans for the expedition had been carefully mapped out. The detachment was to travel by lanes and byroads as much as possible, and under the cover of darkness they hoped to avoid observation and comment. Their chief hope of success lay in taking the enemy by surprise, and every precaution was observed to prevent any miscarriage of their plans.

"Say, fellows, if we can only have the old scout with us by to-morrow night!" exclaimed Frank, turning to his two comrades, his eyes alight with eagerness.

"Wouldn't it be bully?" cried Bart.

"I'm betting that we shall," said Billy hopefully. "That is, if he happens to be the prisoner that Dick was telling us about. Of course that's only a guess."

The order came to fall in, and with Lieutenant Winter at the head the expedition started out on its long hike. The men moved along in loose formation, and all loud talking in the ranks or unnecessary noise was put under the ban.

The night was clear and cold. There was no moon, for which the boys were thankful. There were no cities along the route, and they passed through the occasional scattered hamlets without attracting much attention. Now and then a dog barked and at times a face could be seen pressed against a window pane. Sometimes a straggling figure was seen on the road, but at the sight of the shadowy body of marching men it discreetly vanished into the fields or woods at the side of the highway.

It was about four o'clock in the morning when they reached the outskirts of the town that was their destination. The lieutenant threw out a cordon of men to guard the roads and intercept any one going to or coming from the place. No fires were built, though in the bitter cold of the early morning they would have been grateful. But the men submitted to this privation without grumbling, and stood about stamping their feet and swinging their arms to keep warm and munching the cold rations that they had brought with them.

Within an hour three Germans had been brought in by the

sentries. Two of them were laborers who were coming from a neighboring hamlet to their work in the town. The other had been intercepted coming from the town on his way to take an early train at a railroad station some three miles away.

The men were questioned by the lieutenant with the aid of an interpreter. The laborers knew nothing, or, if they did, they were too frightened by the sight of the armed men about them to answer intelligently. They knew that there had been rioting in the town and some people had been killed and wounded, but they had gone along doing their work and had not been molested. They knew nothing about any American prisoner. They were plainly what they claimed to be and the questioning was not continued long.

The other man proved more intelligent and more communicative. Yes, the Spartacides held possession of the town and the red flag was flying from the town hall. The regular authorities had been disarmed and were held as hostages by the rioters. There had been a good deal of looting of shops and robbery of the homes of the well-to-do.

As to there being any American among the prisoners or hostages, he did not know. He had heard some rumors to that effect, but he had not inquired, for in these days it was well not to show too much curiosity, and he was a quiet man and wanted to keep out of trouble.

The lieutenant was not satisfied that he had told all he knew, and pressed the man further. Under questioning, at first persuasive and then threatening, the man remembered that there had been a meeting of the Spartacides the night before in which the matter of disposing of the prisoners had been discussed. Some had been in favor of executing them out of hand. Others had objected. He did not know what decision had been reached.

Under pressure, he admitted that several executions had already taken place. Where? At the parade ground. Where was that? Not ten minutes walk from where they were now standing. Would he lead them to it?

At this he demurred. He was a peaceful citizen. He did not want to get tangled up in any political affair. He was strictly neutral. The Spartacides would take his life.

A cold glint came into the lieutenant's eyes and his hand dropped carelessly on the handle of his revolver. He toyed with it for a moment. Was the man quite sure that he did not want to show him where the parade ground was?

The man wilted on the instant. Certainly he would show them. He would go that minute if the Herr Lieutenant was ready.

"Very well," said the lieutenant, and promptly gave the order that the men should fall in line, and prepare to march.

In less than ten minutes they were at the designated spot. It was a bleak, wind-swept space of ground, rectangular in shape, on the edge of a stretch of wood. At the end of the grounds nearest the woods there was a blank wall about ten feet high.

As he caught sight of the wall, Frank gave an involuntary shiver that was not from cold.

"What's the matter?" asked Billy Waldon, looking curiously at his companion.

"Nothing," replied Frank Sheldon, studiously avoiding his comrade's eye.

CHAPTER XIX

TURNING THE TABLES

The lieutenant carefully disposed his men in the shelter of the trees and waited.

It was growing a little lighter now that the dawn was beginning to glimmer in the eastern sky.

In a little building at the side of the parade ground lights began to show and figures could be seen passing to and fro. The bustle increased as the moments passed until it could be surmised that something unusual was on foot.

A file of men could be seen going through the dim street on the further side of the building and passing into it by what was evidently the front entrance. Then, after a while, groups of two or three came out through the back door and hung about, smoking, as though they were waiting until the business inside, whatever it was, should be finished.

Most of the men had old German Army uniforms, but others were dressed as civilians. One man wore an officer's cap, but if that really indicated his rank, it was evident from the free and easy way in which he mingled with the others that the old discipline of the German Army had disappeared. The boys remembered that one tenet of the Spartacides' creed was that officer and man should stand on equal terms.

Presently a table was brought out by some men and placed on the ground a little way away from the bottom of the steps. Following this came three men who seemed to be in authority, and behind them a number of prisoners, guarded by men with rifles.

It had grown lighter now, and a thrill went through the Army Boys crouching in their covert as they saw that one of the prisoners wore the American uniform. He was facing the men who sat at the table, evidently his judges, and his back was toward the eyes that were watching him so eagerly from the wood, but they knew in an instant who it was.

It was Tom, dear old Tom, his form as erect, his bearing as defiant as they had always known it! They knew that figure too well to be mistaken. There was a constriction in their throats and their hands gripped their rifles until it seemed as if their fingers would bury themselves in the stocks.

They were at too great a distance to hear what was said, but it was apparent that a trial of some kind was in progress. It might have been that some of them had scruples about executing the prisoners out of hand, and the form was observed in order to get their assent to the bloody work that the majority had determined on.

But that the trial was a mere form was evident from the hurried way in which it was carried on. One by one, the prisoners, of whom there seemed to be about a dozen, passed before the table, were asked a few questions, and then dismissed to take their stand on the other side. It was pitiful to note that one or two of the prisoners were mere boys, while others were men well advanced in years. One, who wore a velvet cap, seemed to be a person of consequence, possibly an official of the town.

Not more than fifteen minutes had passed before all had gone through this mockery of a trial. It was evident that their fate was predetermined, for none was freed. All took their places between the guards and awaited the next move of the men who held in their hands the power of life and death.

During all this time the eyes of the Army Boys had been glued on the one figure of their comrade. They had noted that of all the prisoners he alone had his hands tied behind him. It filled them with pride to see the undaunted way in which he had faced his captors and the evident scorn with which he had heard his fate. While some of the prisoners were weeping, others wringing their hands, and others standing in an attitude of completest dejection, he was apparently as self-possessed and unalarmed as though he had been standing in front of the barracks at Ehrenbreitstein.

"Same old Tom!" whispered Frank to Bart. "The Germans never cowed him yet."

"He's faced death too many times to fear it now," answered Bart, with a catching of his breath. "They knew, too, what they were about when they tied his hands."

"You bet they know what those hands can do," added Billy.

Two or three minutes elapsed while a dispute seemed to be going on between the men seated at the table. Then, at a given signal, the guards marshaled the prisoners in line and led them toward the wall at the back of the parade ground.

The Army Boys were in a fever of apprehension.

Homer Randall

"What's the lieutenant doing?" asked Bart impatiently. "Can't he see that now's the time?"

"Don't worry," admonished Frank, though he himself was frantic with the desire for action. "He knows what he's about."

The prisoners were lined up in a row about ten feet from the wall. Then by a refinement of cruelty, spades were brought forward, and the condemned men were bidden to dig their own graves. The guards passed along the line, placing a spade in the hand of each and telling them roughly what they were to do. They came to Tom and saw that his hands were bound. There was hesitation and a moment's colloquy between two of the guards, and then one of them drew his knife and cut the cords while the other handed Tom a spade.

Tom took it.

The next instant he had whirled it over his head and brought it down on the head of the guard nearest him. The man went down as if shot. Spinning about, Tom sent the other guard down in a heap. Then he hurled the improvised weapon into the ranks of the men's comrades, who in wild excitement were bringing their rifles to their shoulders, and broke like a deer toward the woods.

"Charge!" shouted Lieutenant Winter.

Never was order obeyed with more alacrity. Out of the woods came rushing the men of the old Thirty-seventh, sending a hail of bullets before them. Several of the German firing squad went down at the first volley and the rest were overborne in the mad rush.

The scene was indescribable. There was a crackling of

scattered shots from the startled Germans. The men who had acted as judges jumped to their feet in terror and tried to escape. Bullets brought down one of them, a bayonet another, while the remaining member of the trio was gripped and held none too gently by enraged doughboys.

In a few minutes it was all over. The prisoners were placed under guard and the Americans were recalled from the chase.

And in the midst of the Army Boys was Tom, panting, spent, breathless, mauled and pounded by his rejoicing comrades, scarcely able to believe in his good fortune—good old Tom, who once more in his adventurous career had gone into the very jaws of death and had come out unscathed!

CHAPTER XX

THE CLAWS OF THE HUNS

There was a wild tumult of questions and answers. None of the Army Boys knew what they were doing or saying. The escape had been so narrow, the relief at deliverance so great, that they were simply incoherent for a while.

"Thank heaven, old man, that we have you with us again safe and sound!" cried Frank, as he grasped his comrade's hand and almost wrung it off.

"I felt as though my heart were going to come out of my body while I watched you," said Bart, gripping the other hand.

"It seemed ages while we stood waiting for the lieutenant to give the word," added Billy, giving vent to his feelings by giving Tom a hug like that of a boa constrictor.

"I don't know yet whether I'm awake or dreaming," said Tom, with a laugh that was a little shaky. "You boys surely did come just in time. I never expected to see you again. And yet I might have known that you'd find me if I was on top of the earth."

"You made a game fight for it, old boy," said Frank admiringly.

"Gee, what a clip you gave those fellows with that spade," chuckled Billy. "They went down like cattle hit with an axe."

"You might have won out even without us," said Bart "If you had once got into those woods they'd have had to do some traveling to catch you."

"They'd probably have caught me with a bullet," laughed Tom. "Can you imagine, boys, how I felt when I saw you fellows fairly seem to come up out of the ground? I hadn't really thought that I had a chance to escape. But I made up my mind that if I had to go I'd take some of those Huns along with me. That spade that they wanted me to dig my grave with was a good friend of mine."

"Where they made a mistake was not digging the grave themselves and letting your hands stay tied," said Billy. "But here comes the lieutenant."

Lieutenant Winter came along the line and greeted Tom warmly.

"Good work you did with that spade, Bradford," he said with a twinkle in his eye. "It simply shows that in fighting it's the man more than the weapon that counts. Well, you're safe with us again, and I'm glad on my own account and for the sake of the regiment. We couldn't afford to lose a good two-fisted fighter like you. As soon as you've been to mess I'll want to see you again and question you on what you've learned while you've been a prisoner."

He passed on to look after the captives and set a guard to maintain order in the town. The ringleaders had been captured, and the rest of the Spartacides were cowed and bewildered. And now, encouraged by the presence of the Americans, the more decent element of the community again asserted themselves and the rioters either fled or went into hiding.

The company cook had been busy foraging, and soon had a hot breakfast ready for the detachment, who after their long vigil in the cold and darkness fell upon it like so many hungry wolves. The Army Boys did their full share, and Tom especially ate ravenously and as though he could never get enough.

"Did they starve you, old boy?" asked Frank, as the food disappeared like magic.

"Starve's the right word," answered Tom, as well as he could with his mouth full. "Didn't get a quarter of what I needed. Watery soup and carrots and black bread and once in a while a musty piece of meat. And it wasn't because they were short of food, for they simply gorged. They just wanted to torture me because they hated all Americans, and I happened to be the only one within their reach. Oh, I just love those gentle Huns. I've come to believe that there are only two classes in the world—human beings and Germans."

"I've known that ever since I saw what they did in France and Belgium," remarked Bart. "No other people on earth could have done it!"

After they had finished their meal Tom received a summons to go to the hall that Lieutenant Winter had selected as his temporary quarters. When he entered the hall he started, for he saw among the men standing there the man whom the lieutenant had captured and used as a guide to the parade ground. The man saw him at the same time and sought to efface himself among the others.

"Do you know that man?" asked the lieutenant, who had seen Tom's start of surprise.

"Only too well," said Tom, in a tone where bitterness and scorn were mingled.

"What about him?" asked the lieutenant.

"He's one of the ringleaders of that gang of highbinders," answered Tom.

The lieutenant looked at the man stonily.

"So you're the peaceful citizen that knew so little about the Spartacides, are you?" he asked bitingly.

The man started to protest, but the lieutenant shut him up brusquely and turned to Tom.

"It's lucky you came in just when you did," he said. "I was just about to let this man go because of his services in showing us where the parade ground was. I know now why he was so reluctant to do it." "He did it to save his own skin," answered Tom. "He's a coward as well as a murderer. He's been responsible for other executions that have taken place here in the last few days. He's been one of the bloodiest of the lot, and whenever he saw one of the gang begin to weaken he's stiffened him up. He started out this morning to go to another town to stir up the same kind of riot and murder. I heard him talking about it last night. And just before he went he came to the room where I was confined and taunted me. Told me that I'd be food for the worms to-morrow and that before long there'd be a lot of Americans to keep me company."

The man again started to protest, but one of the doughboys who was on guard gripped him by the collar and dug his knuckles into his neck as he yanked him back.

"Take him away and put him in the same cell where Bradford was held," commanded the lieutenant. "He shall have a taste of his own medicine. He'll get a trial when he gets to Coblenz, and the chances are that he'll face a firing squad. Such fiendish work as he's been doing is going to be stopped if it takes the whole American army to do it!"

The eyes of the Americans followed the cringing figure of the German as he was led away, and then the lieutenant turned to Tom.

"Now for your story, Bradford," he said, and took a pen and prepared to jot down the main points of the former prisoner's experience.

CHAPTER XXI

SQUARING ACCOUNTS

Tom told in detail just what had happened since he had fallen into the hands of the Huns. He had been taken from place to place and treated with the greatest harshness. Everywhere he had witnessed scenes of bloodshed and cruelty. The Spartacides had spared neither age nor sex. They had seemed possessed with a lust for murder. Their bloody work had a fit emblem in their red flag. Tom's familiarity with the language had not been great enough to understand all that was said in the conferences that he frequently overheard, though he had picked up enough to know that murder and riot were being planned on an extensive scale in the district occupied by the American Army. Some of the Germans in the mob had lived previously in America, from which they came to serve in the German Army when war had been declared and while the United States was still neutral, and these men, Tom said, were among the bitterest of all. Often in their off hours they would come and stand in front of his cell and tell him blood curdling stories of what they had been doing and of what they were going to do to him also. They had spoken freely, for they regarded him as good as dead, and some of the information he had gained from the talk of these miscreants was regarded as of great value by the lieutenant, whose pen fairly flew over the paper at some points in Tom's narrative.

At last Tom had told the lieutenant all he knew, and after thanking him the officer dismissed him.

He was witness to some touching sights as he made his way back to his companions. There were mothers embracing their sons, wives weeping with joy in the arms of their husbands who had been Tom's companions in the grim march that morning to the rear wall where they were to face death. But there were no fresh stains on that wall this morning, and the graves remained undug, though here and there were seen the first marks of spades where the wretched victims had begun to dig. It had been a close call, and Tom involuntarily shuddered. The cool air that he drew into his lungs had never seemed so sweet to him as now.

He found the Army Boys looking with great interest at a spade which they held out to him as they approached.

"Here's a souvenir, old boy," grinned Billy.

"It's the one you lammed into the Huns with," explained Bart. "My, but that was a mighty wallop. They went down like tenpins."

"I guess it gave them a headache," laughed Tom. "I know that I put all my weight behind the blows."

"One of them will never have any more headaches," declared Frank. "Even his thick German skull wasn't proof against that blow. Subsequent proceedings will interest him no more."

"The other one was taken to the hospital with a broken shoulder," remarked Billy.

"If Tom had only had time, he'd have cleaned out the whole

bunch," laughed Bart. "As it is, he's given them a wholesome respect for American muscle."

"And American speed too, I imagine," grinned Billy. "The way Tom was making for the woods was a caution. A jack rabbit had nothing on him."

They could joke about the matter now, but it had been far from a joke at that moment not far removed, when life and death had been trembling in the balance.

"Tell us how we came to lose you, Tom," said Frank, as he threw down the spade and they made their way to their temporary quarters. "One minute we saw you and the next we didn't."

"You vanished like a ghost," put in Bart "When we were fighting in that house I saw you knock down one of the rioters with the butt of your gun. I was busy myself then with a husky roughneck, but I tumbled him over and looked around for you and couldn't see you."

"We thought at first," said Billy, "that you might have fallen between the houses when you were chasing the Huns over the roof. We made a careful search afterward, but couldn't find hide nor hair of you. You weren't in any of the hospitals, either. You seemed to have melted into thin air."

"I'm blest if I know myself how it happened," said Tom. "The last I remember was that a couple tackled me at once. I lunged my bayonet at one of them, and then I must have gone down and out, although I don't even remember being hit. I suppose, though, that the other fellow caught me a clip with a gun butt, for when I next knew anything I had a lump on the back of my head as big as an egg.

"I found myself in an attic that was as black as Egypt," he went on. "I couldn't tell whether it was day or night, for there didn't seem to be any window. My hands were tied behind me, and I was aching from head to foot. After a while a bunch of Huns came in, took me downstairs, and pitched me into a covered wagon. Then they drove off into the country. Where they took me I don't know, but after a long ride I was taken out of the wagon and slammed down in a room of what seemed to be a deserted cabin. I only knew it was somewhere in the woods, for through the windows I could see trees all around.

"After a while two or three men who seemed to be the leaders came in. One of them, who could speak English, tried to put me through the third degree. They wanted me to tell them all that I knew about the army forces in Coblenz and the surrounding districts, how many there were, where they were located, what the plans were, and all that kind of dope. Of course I didn't know anything, and then they took it out of me in kicks. I got lots of them, and I guess I'm black and blue all over. They're a plucky lot when a man's hands are tied."

There was a murmur of rage and sympathy from his comrades and their fists clenched.

"Some of them wanted to put an end to me right then and there," Tom continued, "but others objected until they could get me a little further into Germany. They felt that the American forces were a little too near for comfort. Great Scott, how they hate the Americans! They fairly frothed at the mouth when they spoke of them. They blame us for their defeat. I've heard them say many a time that if it hadn't been for us they'd have been in Paris long ago and maybe in London."

"I guess they were pretty near right at that," remarked Frank.

"They surely were," agreed Billy. "Your Uncle Samuel came along just in the nick of time."

"But go ahead, Tom," urged Bart. "What did they do with you after that?"

"Just about the same, only more so," replied Tom, with a grin. "I was taken from one town to another until they finally settled down here. They seemed to find it a promising place to carry out their program of loot and murder. There was some pretty sharp street fighting here for a few days, and then the Spartacides got the upper hand and commenced killing some of their hostages. What you saw this morning has been going on for some time, only this was the biggest batch they have had yet. Going to make a grand wind-up as it were. They haven't spared the women, either. One of them was killed yesterday."

"The hounds!" gritted Frank between his teeth.

CHAPTER XXII

WILL THE GERMANS SIGN?

"It was a pitiful sight," said Tom, continuing the tale of his experience while a captive. "One of the women wanted to write a message of farewell to her husband and children. They gave her paper and pencil, and one of the guards offered his back to rest the paper on while she wrote. At about every sentence, the guard let himself fall down and the woman stumbled over him. It was great fun for the rest of the gang. They laughed as if it were a show. Oh, I tell you, the Huns are great humorists!"

The eyes of the Army Boys flashed.

"The unspeakable beasts!" cried Frank.

"It would be a good thing if a plague came along and snuffed out the whole nation!" angrily exclaimed Bart.

"It might be a good thing for the rest of the world," agreed Tom. "And, by the way, speaking of plague, I don't know but what it's on the way even now. In one or two of the places I've been in there's a mysterious something that's killing off the people like sheep. I've heard the guards talking about it. Nobody seems to know what it is and the doctors themselves are all at sea. Only yesterday one of the guards was taken with it. Big husky fellow he was too, and yet in a couple of hours he was dead. Seems to work as quickly as the cholera and to be just as deadly. I hope it doesn't hit the American Army."

"It has hit it already," replied Frank soberly. "There's quite a lot of our boys in Coblenz who have died of it, and the officers are all up in the air about it. The medical staff is at its wit's end. I tell you, it's getting to be a mighty big problem."

"I wish we were out of the hoodooed country!" exclaimed Bart savagely. "The whole land seems to rest under a curse. When on earth will that treaty be signed so that we can go back to the States?"

"The Germans say that they're not going to sign it if it proves to be as severe as is reported," remarked Tom. "I've heard that said on every side."

"'They say' they're not," sneered Billy. "What does their 'they say' amount to? Nothing at all. They said they'd never stop fighting, and they lay down like dogs. They said we'd never step on the sacred soil of Germany, but there wasn't a peep out of them when we marched over the Rhine. They're the biggest bluffers and the quickest quitters in the world."

"When are we going back to Coblenz?" asked Tom.

"In a hurry to get back are you?" laughed Frank. "Well, I don't blame you, old man. Billy tells me that Alice has been crying her pretty eyes out ever since you disappeared. But I suppose we'll have to hang around here for a few days yet. There's a lot to be done in cleaning out the Spartacides and getting the town in proper condition. The lieut. won't go back till he's finished the job. But you needn't worry, for by this time he's telephoned the whole thing over to Coblenz, and the authorities there know that you're safe and sound. It's a safe bet that Alice has already learned the good news."

Frank's conjecture turned out to be correct, for it was nearly a week before the lieutenant concluded that his work in the town was done. Then the column took up its march in a jubilant mood, for their comrade, who was a prime favorite in the regiment, had been rescued and the work had been done in the deft and finished way that marked the traditions of the American Army.

Tom and Billy slipped away as soon as they could obtain leave after they reached the city, and there was not any doubt in any one's mind as to their destination. Nor on their return to the barracks that night, bubbling over with glee and high spirits, was there any question but that their visit had been a thoroughly satisfactory one. If traces of his captivity were still visible in Tom's rather hollow cheeks and shrunken waistband, they had entirely disappeared from his manner.

His comrades had of course told him of their adventure in connection with the trap door, and he was all agog with interest in their recital of their battle with the rats, scars of whose bites were still visible as evidence if any had been necessary.

"It must have been some fight!" he remarked, with a touch of envy. "Gee! I'd like to have been with you. Too bad, though, that you didn't find out what you went after. Of course you're not going to give it up?"

"You bet your life we're not!" answered Frank emphatically. "Give it up isn't in our dictionary. We're going to search that place again, rats or no rats, only the next time we'll have clubs and be ready for them."

"That's the way to talk!" cried Tom. "That'll give me a chance to get in on the game."

"I don't know that the rats will trouble us next time," put in Billy. "You'll remember that it was only after we got past that place where the light was that we came across them in any numbers. Their stamping ground seemed to be further on."

"That seems likely enough," agreed Bart. "The light being there showed that somebody had been using the passage without hindrance. We simply had the hard luck to get in the quarter where the rats were thickest. At any rate, well take another chance."

That chance was not as soon in coming as they had hoped for, however, for Coblenz was now seething with unrest. The disorders that were prevalent all over Germany were manifesting themselves in the region of the Rhine. Scarcely a day passed without an outrage of some kind being reported. Several American soldiers were found stabbed in the street by unknown assassins. Agitators from Berlin were slipping into the city and trying to stir up insurrection. It was feared that the sharp lesson given on a previous occasion would have to be repeated.

Strikes were called in various industries, and sullen knots of idle men, ripe for mischief, were in evidence everywhere. When they were dispersed by military patrols, it was only to gather in some other place.

CHAPTER XXIII

ON THE VERGE OF DISCOVERY

In view of the menacing situation and the black looks and muttered curses that were thrown at the Americans who were policing the city, military regulations were tightened. Leaves of absence were either forbidden or greatly curtailed, and the Army Boys found themselves confined to their barracks when not actually on service. So the projected trip to the alley had to be deferred.

Weeks passed by and lengthened into months. Winter had disappeared and spring had come, bringing with it soft breezes and verdant fields and budding flowers and clothing the valley of the Rhine in beauty.

It was a welcome change to the Army Boys, who had chafed over the forced inaction and abstention from outdoor sports caused by the severe winter. Now most of the time off duty was spent in the open, and baseball and other games made the banishment from home seem less of a hardship. Company teams were organized and there was a good deal of healthy rivalry between the various nines. The Army Boys were expert players, and the work they did on the diamond speedily placed their nine in the lead.

But underneath all their work and fun lay the longing for home. They were in an alien country, among a people that hated them, a people bitter from defeat and eager for revenge.

They flung themselves down on the river bank one afternoon to rest after an unusually exciting game of ball when they had just managed to nose out their opponents in the ninth inning.

"Beautiful river, isn't it?" remarked Frank, his eyes following the windings of the Rhine, visible there for many miles in either direction.

"Oh, the country's pretty enough," conceded Bart grudgingly. "It's the people in it that I object to."

"'Where every prospect pleases,
And only man is vile,'"

quoted Billy.

"I wish the Paris Conference would get busy and finish up that treaty," observed Frank impatiently. "What in heck keeps them dawdling so long over it?"

"It's like a sewing circle," grumbled Bart. "There's a lot of talk and mighty little work done."

"We'll be doddering old men by the time they get through," added Tom.

"Time seems to be no object with them," commented Billy.

"Of course," admitted Frank, "I suppose there's an awful lot to do. The world's been ripped wide open by these pesky

Huns, and it's some job to sew it up again. Still it does seem that they ought to hustle things a good deal more than they are doing. I'm anxious to shake the dust of Germany from my feet forever."

"What's the latest you've heard about the peace terms?" Billy inquired.

"Oh, Germany's going to get hers, all right," replied Frank grimly. "She's had her dance, and now she's going to pay the piper. She's going to lose her colonies, for one thing. She won't have a single foot of land outside of Germany itself, and a lot of that's going to be cut away from her, too. Alsace-Lorraine of course goes back to France. Schleswig, that Bismarck stole, will be given to Denmark. The Poles will get part of East and West Prussia, Posen and Silesia. The coal mines in the Sarre Basin go to France, to make up for the destruction of French coal mines at Lens. Germany's got to give back ton for ton the shipping sunk by her submarines. She must yield up all her aircraft, and can keep an army of only one hundred thousand men. Then, too, she'll have to fork over a little trifle of forty or fifty billion dollars, an amount that will keep her nose to the grindstone for the next thirty years. Oh, yes, Germany will pay the piper all right."

"It isn't enough," said Bart curtly.

"No," put in Billy. "She's getting off too easily. That's only sticking a knife in hen. They ought to twist the knife around."

"Even with all that," declared Tom, "she won't begin to pay for all the misery and death she caused. But what are they going to do with the Kaiser?" he continued. "Have you heard about that?"

"Oh, they're talking about yanking him out of Holland and putting him on trial," answered Frank; "but it's a gamble if they really will. He's such a skulking cowardly figure just now that perhaps it wouldn't be well to try him. It might dignify him too much, make a martyr of him. They may let him and the Crown Prince stay where they are. There's no telling."

"Well," remarked Tom, as they rose to their feet and started toward the barracks, "whatever the terms, I only hope they'll hurry them up and let us get back to the States."

A week of comparative quiet followed, and the situation in Coblenz seemed to be well in hand. That is, as far as disturbances were concerned. The mysterious disease, however, still seemed to be uncurbed, despite all the efforts of the medical staff.

Military restrictions now were somewhat relaxed. Leaves of absence were more easily obtained, but it was some time before the Army Boys were able to arrange things so that all their leaves fell on the same night.

That time came at last, however, and they started out soon after nightfall with the determination once for all to solve the mystery of the alley. The night was extremely dark, and as the moon would not rise till late they had comparatively little difficulty in seizing an opportunity when the street was practically deserted to slip into the alley unobserved.

Their task was rendered easier by the fact that there was no longer ice to hinder their raising of the trap door. It creaked under the straining of their arms, but it yielded, and, using the utmost caution, they descended into the yawning chasm.

They had provided themselves with stout sticks that they felt sure would enable them to ward off any attack by rats, though they devoutly hoped that these would not be needed. Nor were they, for Billy's conjecture that the part infested by them was beyond the lighted corridor proved correct.

With the stealth of Indians they moved along the narrow passage, darting glances into every opening that seemed to branch off from the main corridor. For some time nothing greeted their eyes but impenetrable blackness, and they began to think that either the light had been extinguished or that they had inadvertently passed it by.

"Hist!" came from Billy's lips, and they halted.

"There it is," he said in a low tone.

They clustered about him as he pointed to the left. There, sure enough, was the electric bulb glowing, and behind it the outline of a door. Turning into the passage and inwardly thankful that as yet no rats had been encountered, they made their way toward the light.

The door, as revealed by the light, was of heavy oak. There was no crack or crevice in it anywhere. Standing close to the door they listened intently for any sound from the other side. Everything was absolutely quiet. All that they could hear was their own excited breathing.

Frank put his hand on the knob of the door and flashed a look of mute inquiry at his comrades. They nodded under-standingly, and inch by inch Frank noiselessly drew the door open.

There was no light in the room beyond, but a ray from the electric bulb outside fell on a row of bottles and retorts that indicated a chemical laboratory.

Frank had drawn his flashlight from his section pocket and was about to turn it upon the room, when suddenly the room became radiant with a perfect flood of light. At the same time there was the sound of a quick step in the hall beyond the room, the click of a door knob, and Frank had just time to push the heavy oaken door nearly to, when the further door opened and a man came into the room.

Through the crack of the door Frank caught a glimpse of the man's face and started back in surprise.

CHAPTER XXIV

THE DEADLY PHIAL

It was the famous physician, the man whose hate for Americans was so notorious, the man with whom they had already had unpleasant encounters, the man who had so often shot venomous looks at Frank and his comrades as they passed and yet who of late had worn an air so jubilant.

It was his house then to which this mysterious passage afforded secret entrance, that entrance which the Army Boys had felt sure was used by conspirators and assassins. What did it all mean?

The doctor approached one of the retorts in which some concoction was bubbling and examined it carefully, reducing the heat a little as he glanced at the thermometer. Then he walked over to a row of phials on one of the shelves and handled them almost caressingly. One of them he pressed with an almost rapturous gesture to his breast, at the same time breaking out in a strain of mingled eulogy and denunciation. The eulogy seemed to be for the phial, the denunciation for the "accursed Americans," which phrase Frank heard him repeat several times.

The doctor then replaced the phials on the shelf and picked

up an evening paper printed in German that was lying on a chair. He looked over the headlines which ran all the way across the page, and indulged in a chuckle. He read the article through, then threw down the paper and walked to and fro in the room, rubbing his hands and evidently in the highest spirits.

The paper had been thrown down in such a way that Frank could plainly see the flaring headlines. They ran thus:

"MYSTERIOUS DISEASE STILL UNABATED More Americans Stricken."

This then accounted for the doctor's elation. Frank's eye glanced from the paper to the phial and back again to the paper.

Suddenly a terrible conviction struck him with the force of a blow.

At that moment a bell rang somewhere outside. The doctor stopped in his pacing, listened a moment, and then with a gesture of impatience strode to the door and passed out into the hall, closing the door after him.

Like a flash, Frank was in the room and had possessed himself of the mysterious phial. Then he was back again among his companions, who had gazed after him in wonder.

"Quick!" he directed as he closed the heavy door. "Back to the alley as fast as we can."

"What's the big idea, Frank?" asked Bart, as the boys hurried after their leader.

"Can't stop to talk about it now, old fellow. Tell you later what I think I've stumbled on. I think I know now what my hunch meant. I'm streaking it straight for headquarters as fast as my legs will carry me."

Bart saw how wrought up he was, and followed him without further questioning.

Straight to his captain Frank hastened and told his story. He had not finished before the captain sent out hastily for others higher in authority. Then Frank, often interrupted by excited questioning, narrated every detail of the night's discovery. The phial was handed over to the chief medical officer, and Frank, after hearty commendation, was bidden to hold himself ready for call at a moment's notice.

He hurried off to the barracks, where his comrades were eagerly awaiting him. To them he poured out all he knew and suspected.

That night and the next day witnessed busy scenes at the headquarters of the medical staff. The contents of the phial were analysed and justified Frank's suspicions. A force was organized in which the Army Boys were included to seize the arch-plotter. It would have been possible to have entered his house from the front, but the broad street on which it stood was a thoroughfare thronged with people at night, and in order to avoid possible riot and attempt at rescue it was deemed best to enter from the trap door in the alley.

As soon as it was fully dark, the detachment was set in motion. Sentries were posted on either side of the alley to prevent any one from entering, and one by one the arresting party swept down through the passage from the alley and they made their way, with Frank as guide, to the oaken door. Here they paused and listened.

Far from being empty, as on the night before, there were sounds in the room that amounted almost to tumult. Loud exclamations were interspersed with bursts of laughter. The main note seemed to be approval. Some one who aroused the enthusiasm of his hearers was speaking.

Slowly, very slowly, Lieutenant Winter, who was in charge, drew the door open by imperceptible degrees. It was the doctor himself who was holding forth, almost with frenzy. His gestures were wild and his words came so fast as to make his speech almost incoherent.

But the listeners caught enough from that wild torrent of words to know that their darkest suspicions were more than justified. The man was gloating over his wickedness, over the deaths that had already resulted, and the deaths he hoped to cause through his diabolical discovery.

He stopped at length, and others in the party had their turn. Here was something beyond what the raiding party had looked for. They had stumbled upon a nest of conspirators who, in their way, as the doctor in his, were deadly enemies of society in general and the Americans in particular.

Through this secret passage into the alley, for how long none of them knew, these desperate men had been going to and fro, avoiding attention and hatching in the doctor's office a plot that had kept the entire zone of the American Army of Occupation in a state of unrest. The proof was all-sufficient, and the conspirators were weaving the noose for their own necks.

The lieutenant lifted his hand, swung the door wide open, and, followed by his men, rushed into the room.

CHAPTER XXV

THE TREATY SIGNED

It was a scene of wild confusion. Men jumped from their seats with shouts and execrations. One man leaped for the electric switch to turn out the light, but Frank reached him at a bound and felled him to the floor. Pistols were drawn, but the doughboys knocked them out of the conspirators' hands, and in a twinkling had the men gripped and powerless.

The doctor crammed some papers into his mouth with the evident intention of swallowing them, but Tom's sinewy hands were at his throat and choked them out.

It was all over in a few moments. The surprise had been so great that resistance was futile. The baffled conspirators stood huddled together, disarmed, and under guard.

The doctor's rage was fearful as his eyes rested on Frank, for whom he had cherished bitter enmity since their first encounter, and who he felt instinctively was the cause of his undoing.

The lieutenant gave a few curt commands and the prisoners were led out through the passage, secret no longer, and conveyed under guard to American headquarters.

Here a number of leading American officers had gathered to await the results of the raid. The prisoners were remanded for examination on the morrow, with the exception of the doctor, who was brought at once before the tribunal and sternly questioned.

At first he remained stubbornly silent, refusing to say a word. Then the crumpled papers that he had attempted to swallow were opened and read.

They proved to be the formulas relating to the deadly germs contained in the phials. Step by step the process was described. The proof was positive and overwhelming. But most important of all was the setting down of the antidote that would neutralize the effect of the germs.

The doctor's face during the reading of the papers was a study in emotions. Rage, disappointment, hate succeeded one another. Upon the faces of his judges the prevalent expression was one of horror, tempered somewhat by the relief afforded by the knowledge that the antidote was within their reach.

Being asked if he had anything to say, the doctor at last broke his stubborn silence. Denial was impossible. The game was up. There was nothing to gain by repressing his feelings, and he broke out in a wild tirade.

Yes, he said, it was true that he had discovered and isolated this deadly germ and had made numberless cultures of it to be spread broadcast. He boasted of it. He gloried in it. He had already killed many of the hated Americans, and if he had been given time he would have swept the whole American Army of Occupation off the face of the earth. It was true that he had not confined his operations to the Americans alone. He had sought revenge on his own cowardly countrymen who had yielded supinely and permitted the Americans to occupy the fairest districts of Germany. He had offered his deadly discovery to the German commanders before the armistice was signed, but either through doubts of its value or fear that their own troops would share in the contagion they had refused to make use of it. Then his rage had turned against countrymen and foes alike. Like Caligula, he had wished that the whole human race had but a single head so that he might cut it off with one blow. He would have done it, too, if this accursed young American—

Here he made a savage lunge at Frank, and there was a terrific struggle before he was overpowered by the guards. He fought with the strength of a maniac, which indeed he was, for the wild rage under which he labored had reached its climax in the overturning of his reason. He was dragged away, struggling, fighting, and foaming at the mouth.

There was unmeasured joy and relief at American head-quarters that night, for the shadow of the plague that had hung over the army for months was lifted and the remedy was known. Frank and his comrades came in for praise and commendation that made their faces glow, and it was promised that promotion and crosses of honor would be a reward and recognition of their splendid work.

And now the date had been set for the signing of the Peace Treaty. Germany was at white heat in protest against the terms. She swore that she would never sign. She raged like a wild beast that had been caught in a trap. With characteristic treachery she sank the interned fleet at Scapa Flow. A mob burned the French flags in Berlin, of which the treaty demanded the surrender. Sign the treaty? Never! Never!

The Americans were ready on the instant to march toward

Berlin. Twenty-four hours before the time set for signing, tanks, airplanes, guns and men poured over the Rhine. If the Germans wanted more fighting they could have it. If they did not sign the treaty at Versailles, they would be compelled to sign it in Berlin. The guns were ready to thunder, the men ready to charge.

The Germans saw those preparations and wilted. Their boasting changed to whining.

On June the twenty-eighth they signed the treaty. *The war was over!*

And when that night the booming of guns at Coblenz told that the treaty had been signed, the Army Boys hugged each other in delight at the knowledge that their work was done and that now they were free to go back home!

"Hurrah!" cried Billy in wild jubilation.

"Back to the States!" shouted Bart.

"Three cheers for Old Glory!" exclaimed Tom.

"And a tiger," added Frank. "Well, fellows, our work is over. Our boys came over here to! whip the Hun. They did it. They came over to help win the war. They did it. The job is done, and now we Army Boys can go back in triumph to God's country!"

THE END

Choose from Thousands of 1stWorldLibrary Classics By

A. M. Barnard
Ada Leverson
Adolphus William Ward
Aesop
Agatha Christie
Alexander Aaronsohn
Alexander Kielland
Alexandre Dumas
Alfred Gatty
Alfred Ollivant
Alice Duer Miller
Alice Turner Curtis
Alice Dunbar
Allen Chapman
Alleyne Ireland
Ambrose Bierce
Amelia E. Barr
Amory H. Bradford
Andrew Lang
Andrew McFarland Davis
Andy Adams
Angela Brazil
Anna Alice Chapin
Anna Sewell
Annie Besant
Annie Hamilton Donnell
Annie Payson Call
Annie Roe Carr
Annonaymous
Anton Chekhov
Archibald Lee Fletcher
Arnold Bennett
Arthur C. Benson
Arthur Conan Doyle
Arthur M. Winfield
Arthur Ransome
Arthur Schnitzler
Arthur Train
Atticus
B.H. Baden-Powell
B. M. Bower
B. C. Chatterjee
Baroness Emmuska Orczy
Baroness Orczy
Basil King
Bayard Taylor
Ben Macomber
Bertha Muzzy Bower
Bjornstjerne Bjornson

Booth Tarkington
Boyd Cable
Bram Stoker
C. Collodi
C. E. Orr
C. M. Ingleby
Carolyn Wells
Catherine Parr Traill
Charles A. Eastman
Charles Amory Beach
Charles Dickens
Charles Dudley Warner
Charles Farrar Browne
Charles Ives
Charles Kingsley
Charles Klein
Charles Hanson Towne
Charles Lathrop Pack
Charles Romyn Dake
Charles Whibley
Charles Willing Beale
Charlotte M. Braeme
Charlotte M. Yonge
Charlotte Perkins Stetson
Clair W. Hayes
Clarence Day Jr.
Clarence E. Mulford
Clemence Housman
Confucius
Coningsby Dawson
Cornelis DeWitt Wilcox
Cyril Burleigh
D. H. Lawrence
Daniel Defoe
David Garnett
Dinah Craik
Don Carlos Janes
Donald Keyhoe
Dorothy Kilner
Dougan Clark
Douglas Fairbanks
E. Nesbit
E. P. Roe
E. Phillips Oppenheim
E. S. Brooks
Earl Barnes
Edgar Rice Burroughs
Edith Van Dyne
Edith Wharton

Edward Everett Hale
Edward J. O'Biren
Edward S. Ellis
Edwin L. Arnold
Eleanor Atkins
Eleanor Hallowell Abbott
Eliot Gregory
Elizabeth Gaskell
Elizabeth McCracken
Elizabeth Von Arnim
Ellem Key
Emerson Hough
Emilie F. Carlen
Emily Bronte
Emily Dickinson
Enid Bagnold
Enilor Macartney Lane
Erasmus W. Jones
Ernie Howard Pie
Ethel May Dell
Ethel Turner
Ethel Watts Mumford
Eugene Sue
Eugenie Foa
Eugene Wood
Eustace Hale Ball
Evelyn Everett-green
Everard Cotes
F. H. Cheley
F. J. Cross
F. Marion Crawford
Fannie E. Newberry
Federick Austin Ogg
Ferdinand Ossendowski
Fergus Hume
Florence A. Kilpatrick
Fremont B. Deering
Francis Bacon
Francis Darwin
Frances Hodgson Burnett
Frances Parkinson Keyes
Frank Gee Patchin
Frank Harris
Frank Jewett Mather
Frank L. Packard
Frank V. Webster
Frederic Stewart Isham
Frederick Trevor Hill
Frederick Winslow Taylor

Friedrich Kerst
Friedrich Nietzsche
Fyodor Dostoyevsky
G.A. Henty
G.K. Chesterton
Gabrielle E. Jackson
Garrett P. Serviss
Gaston Leroux
George A. Warren
George Ade
Geroge Bernard Shaw
George Cary Eggleston
George Durston
George Ebers
George Eliot
George Gissing
George MacDonald
George Meredith
George Orwell
George Sylvester Viereck
George Tucker
George W. Cable
George Wharton James
Gertrude Atherton
Gordon Casserly
Grace E. King
Grace Gallatin
Grace Greenwood
Grant Allen
Guillermo A. Sherwell
Gulielma Zollinger
Gustav Flaubert
H. A. Cody
H. B. Irving
H. C. Bailey
H. G. Wells
H. H. Munro
H. Irving Hancock
H. R. Naylor
H. Rider Haggard
H. W. C. Davis
Haldeman Julius
Hall Caine
Hamilton Wright Mabie
Hans Christian Andersen
Harold Avery
Harold McGrath
Harriet Beecher Stowe
Harry Castlemon
Harry Coghill
Harry Houidini

Hayden Carruth
Helent Hunt Jackson
Helen Nicolay
Hendrik Conscience
Hendy David Thoreau
Henri Barbusse
Henrik Ibsen
Henry Adams
Henry Ford
Henry Frost
Henry James
Henry Jones Ford
Henry Seton Merriman
Henry W Longfellow
Herbert A. Giles
Herbert Carter
Herbert N. Casson
Herman Hesse
Hildegard G. Frey
Homer
Honore De Balzac
Horace B. Day
Horace Walpole
Horatio Alger Jr.
Howard Pyle
Howard R. Garis
Hugh Lofting
Hugh Walpole
Humphry Ward
Ian Maclaren
Inez Haynes Gillmore
Irving Bacheller
Isabel Cecilia Williams
Isabel Hornibrook
Israel Abrahams
Ivan Turgenev
J. G.Austin
J. Henri Fabre
J. M. Barrie
J. M. Walsh
J. Macdonald Oxley
J. R. Miller
J. S. Fletcher
J. S. Knowles
J. Storer Clouston
J. W. Duffield
Jack London
Jacob Abbott
James Allen
James Andrews
James Baldwin

James Branch Cabell
James DeMille
James Joyce
James Lane Allen
James Lane Allen
James Oliver Curwood
James Oppenheim
James Otis
James R. Driscoll
Jane Abbott
Jane Austen
Jane L. Stewart
Janet Aldridge
Jens Peter Jacobsen
Jerome K. Jerome
Jessie Graham Flower
John Buchan
John Burroughs
John Cournos
John F. Kennedy
John Gay
John Glasworthy
John Habberton
John Joy Bell
John Kendrick Bangs
John Milton
John Philip Sousa
John Taintor Foote
Jonas Lauritz Idemil Lie
Jonathan Swift
Joseph A. Altsheler
Joseph Carey
Joseph Conrad
Joseph E. Badger Jr
Joseph Hergesheimer
Joseph Jacobs
Jules Vernes
Julian Hawthrone
Julie A Lippmann
Justin Huntly McCarthy
Kakuzo Okakura
Karle Wilson Baker
Kate Chopin
Kenneth Grahame
Kenneth McGaffey
Kate Langley Bosher
Kate Langley Bosher
Katherine Cecil Thurston
Katherine Stokes
L. A. Abbot
L. T. Meade

L. Frank Baum
Latta Griswold
Laura Dent Crane
Laura Lee Hope
Laurence Housman
Lawrence Beasley
Leo Tolstoy
Leonid Andreyev
Lewis Carroll
Lewis Sperry Chafer
Lilian Bell
Lloyd Osbourne
Louis Hughes
Louis Joseph Vance
Louis Tracy
Louisa May Alcott
Lucy Fitch Perkins
Lucy Maud Montgomery
Luther Benson
Lydia Miller Middleton
Lyndon Orr
M. Corvus
M. H. Adams
Margaret E. Sangster
Margret Howth
Margaret Vandercook
Margaret W. Hungerford
Margret Penrose
Maria Edgeworth
Maria Thompson Daviess
Mariano Azuela
Marion Polk Angellotti
Mark Overton
Mark Twain
Mary Austin
Mary Catherine Crowley
Mary Cole
Mary Hastings Bradley
Mary Roberts Rinehart
Mary Rowlandson
M. Wollstonecraft Shelley
Maud Lindsay
Max Beerbohm
Myra Kelly
Nathaniel Hawthrone
Nicolo Machiavelli
O. F. Walton
Oscar Wilde

Owen Johnson
P.G. Wodehouse
Paul and Mabel Thorne
Paul G. Tomlinson
Paul Severing
Percy Brebner
Percy Keese Fitzhugh
Peter B. Kyne
Plato
Quincy Allen
R. Derby Holmes
R. L. Stevenson
R. S. Ball
Rabindranath Tagore
Rahul Alvares
Ralph Bonehill
Ralph Henry Barbour
Ralph Victor
Ralph Waldo Emmerson
Rene Descartes
Ray Cummings
Rex Beach
Rex E. Beach
Richard Harding Davis
Richard Jefferies
Richard Le Gallienne
Robert Barr
Robert Frost
Robert Gordon Anderson
Robert L. Drake
Robert Lansing
Robert Lynd
Robert Michael Ballantyne
Robert W. Chambers
Rosa Nouchette Carey
Rudyard Kipling
Saint Augustine
Samuel B. Allison
Samuel Hopkins Adams
Sarah Bernhardt
Sarah C. Hallowell
Selma Lagerlof
Sherwood Anderson
Sigmund Freud
Standish O'Grady
Stanley Weyman
Stella Benson
Stella M. Francis

Stephen Crane
Stewart Edward White
Stijn Streuvels
Swami Abhedananda
Swami Parmananda
T. S. Ackland
T. S. Arthur
The Princess Der Ling
Thomas A. Janvier
Thomas A Kempis
Thomas Anderton
Thomas Bailey Aldrich
Thomas Bulfinch
Thomas De Quincey
Thomas Dixon
Thomas H. Huxley
Thomas Hardy
Thomas More
Thornton W. Burgess
U. S. Grant
Upton Sinclair
Valentine Williams
Various Authors
Vaughan Kester
Victor Appleton
Victor G. Durham
Victoria Cross
Virginia Woolf
Wadsworth Camp
Walter Camp
Walter Scott
Washington Irving
Wilbur Lawton
Wilkie Collins
Willa Cather
Willard F. Baker
William Dean Howells
William le Queux
W. Makepeace Thackeray
William W. Walter
William Shakespeare
Winston Churchill
Yei Theodora Ozaki
Yogi Ramacharaka
Young E. Allison
Zane Grey